WINDOW of Time

The Stained-Glass Legacy • Book Four

Erin R. Howard

Published by Expanse Books,
an imprint of Scrivenings Press LLC
15 Lucky Lane
Morrilton, Arkansas 72110
https://ExpanseBooks.pub

Printed in the United States of America

Paperback ISBN 978-1-64917-349-2

eBook ISBN 978-1-64917-351-5

Editors: Ann Harrison and Linda Fulkerson

Cover by Linda Fulkerson, bookmarketinggraphics.com

This is a work of fiction. Unless otherwise indicated, all names, characters, businesses, events, and incidents are either the product of the author's imagination or used in a fictitious manner. Any resemblance to actual persons, living or dead, or actual events is purely coincidental.

*To Heather, Amy, and Regina. Three of the best writing sisters that
a girl could ever want.*

Chapter One

The sharp jab of a bobby pin poked the back of Mia Miller's ear as she looked away from her sister's wedding photographer. If she had to listen to the woman's chirpy voice telling them to "smile for June!" one more time, she would fling off the ridiculously high heels that June insisted she wear. She shifted her weight to her left leg. Oh, how she longed to slide into her favorite pair of Converse. A grin spread across her face at the thought. Who would know? Her lavender dress was long enough to cover up the sneakers.

The photographer moved the bridal party into a new pose, and Mia wished she could hide in the back of the wedding chapel in their quaint Tennessee town and watch from afar. She wasn't jealous of her sister and Mark—just reluctant to let Mark into their family bubble.

But one quick glance in her sister's direction brought a wave of guilt. June radiated with joy. She couldn't deny anything that made her sister that happy—so she'd plaster on a smile and keep trudging forward.

Sore feet and all.

Turning away from the happy couple, she brushed away unbidden tears. Now wasn't the time to get so sappy. A rainbow of colors danced across the wooden floor and drew her attention from her thoughts to the beautiful stained-glass window. It was the first thing she noticed when they arrived at the chapel. The way the light filtered through the window drew her closer to get a better look at the unique pattern. Reaching out, she gently traced the etched lines of the glass. Each gentle pass over a new color coaxed the desire to create something new from nothing.

"June, let's sign up for a stained-glass class. It can't be that hard—" She turned, and a flash of light nearly blinded her. "Not another picture."

The photographer lowered the camera with a sheepish expression, but June waved her hand in dismissal. "Oh, please. You always look beautiful, and the lighting was gorgeous behind you."

"Mr. and Mrs. Pierce, it's time to move to the reception." The photographer picked up her camera bag and ushered the bridal party down the aisle toward the door.

A giggle came from her sister's direction. "Mia, don't forget your flowers."

Mia followed June's gesture to the front pew. Her bouquet of daises was exactly where she laid them. "I see them. You guys go on, and I will be right there."

"You sure?" June hesitated but couldn't fully pull her eyes away from Mark.

She was the last Miller. A family of one. How could her heart be full of joy for her sister but sadness too? "Of course. I'll be out to the car in a minute."

"Okay, hurry!"

Her fingers slipped on the silky ribbon before connecting with the bouquet stem as a flicker of light caught her eye at the window. No, not a flicker—more like a shimmer—like the entire window was glowing.

She walked over to it and peered out, searching for the light's source. Mia stood on her tiptoes and craned her neck to get a better view of the sky. The setting sun had already muted the beautiful reflections of light on the floor, so there must be another reason for the bright flickering light.

If anyone walked into the chapel now, they would certainly question her sanity. She sighed, lowered her feet to the ground, and instantly regretted it. Her ankle wobbled in the high heel, throwing off her balance. Without thinking, Mia stuck her empty hand out to brace herself, but her hand didn't touch the window.

It went through it.

Mia's body pitched forward and fell completely through the window. Gasping, she forced her eyes closed and braced for the impact.

Except nothing happened. There was no shattering of glass or pain.

Slowly, Mia opened one eye and then the other, afraid she would see the window in front of her and that somehow her mind had made up the whole thing. But the window *wasn't* in front of her. She whirled around, taking in the room and comparing it to what it had looked like moments before.

The chapel walls were the same. Wooden pews still sat in the same place, but cracked in sections, sagging, and covered with a coat of thick dust. The front of the chapel was an exact replica—just rundown—and the pulpit was missing.

It was like she simply stepped through the window into an older, dirtier version of the chapel, which was completely crazy.

Or was it?

Mia couldn't discredit what was right in front of her, which meant there had to be some sort of logical explanation. She just had to figure out what was happening so she could return to *her* chapel. Her stomach churned at the thought of her sister wondering where she was. June would be beside herself with worry.

Gathering a corner of her silk dress, she lifted it up so the hem wouldn't drag on the dusty floor and turned to go back through the glass.

Except the beautiful stained-glass window was gone.

There was nothing there—just an empty frame and a middle-aged woman staring at her with her mouth halfway open. How long had the woman stood on the other side of the window and watched her? Did she see Mia fall through it? Surely not.

The lady continued to gape at her, so Mia self-consciously raised a hand to pat her hair, making sure the bobby pins still neatly secured her up do. Her blonde curls tended to have a mind of their own, and she didn't trust the bobby pins to hold them. The woman's gaze followed Mia's hand all the way up to her hair, then back down at her feet. Mia took a few seconds to realize she still gripped part of the fabric, showing off her three-inch heels. She released the dress and gave the woman a small wave.

A slow smile spread across the lady's face. "There you are!"

It was Mia's turn to look shocked. "Excuse me?"

The woman raised her hand to her ear and said, "Sir, I've found her."

Panic knotted Mia's stomach at the words. Surely, this stranger didn't mean her. Every instinct she possessed urged her to bolt. She turned around to run but remembered the flowers. She couldn't leave them behind.

"Princess Amelia, what are you doing in here? I was supposed to meet you at the castle courtyard." The lady leaned into the window frame and sighed. "And where are your guards? Your entourage?"

Princess? Castle? Courtyard? Where was she? Better yet—this lady was the one that was crazy. "I think you have the wrong person." Mia somehow formed a coherent sentence and reached for the flowers.

The woman raised her eyebrow and pointed. "Stay right there."

She looked out the window and wished she hadn't. Mia definitely wasn't in Park Haven. There were no grass or trees. No late summer picturesque view of the woods. In their places were neglected buildings, built close together. If she wasn't in her small rural Tennessee town, then where was she?

A long squeal at the front of the chapel drew Mia's gaze. The woman pushed the front door open, and it scraped across the floor. Mia lifted her dress once more and stuck her leg through the window.

She must have gone completely mad because none of this was happening. She was not about to escape out of a window in a formal gown.

"Princess Amelia!"

Ignoring the woman's cries, Mia climbed through the window and sat on the ledge. At least it wasn't much of a leap down. At the last second, she remembered her heels and scooped them off before jumping to the wooden boardwalk below.

A cloud of dust engulfed her, and she waved it away, choking on the heavy air.

"Princess, what are you doing?" Anger and frustration lined the lady's words. This woman really thought Mia was a princess. This was absurd.

"I'm sorry." Mia coughed again and took off down the sidewalk toward a crowd. Hopefully, escaping would buy her some time to hide and gather her thoughts. She had to make this woman understand she wasn't who she was looking for, but she did not know what to say. Telling her she fell through a window didn't exactly sound like the best way to go about it.

Mia slowed her sprint as she neared the crowd. Understanding the woman's confusion suddenly made sense. She was a refreshing splash of color in a sea of muddy water. Shades of muted blues, grays, and browns filled the streets. Gone were the pretty fields and woods of the chapel, the neat little neighborhoods, and quaint downtown shops.

Tears filled her eyes as she looked around the square. People greeted each other, but not in the way she was accustomed to.

Instead of handshakes or hugs, they placed their hand over the heart and bowed their heads.

This was not her town and clearly not her time.

Mia reached up to swipe away the tears when she noticed her shoes dangling from her fingertips. She must be a sight to behold.

A push came from behind, and Mia turned just in time to lock eyes with a girl who appeared to be about her age. The young woman quickly lowered her gaze, bowing over and over as she backed away from her. Mia needed to get out of this crowd before the girl brought more attention toward her.

Mia darted across the street, ducking into the first booth she found with long, rough fabric hanging in the opening. She let it close behind her, but she clung to it as if it would help her make sense of what was happening. A gasp filled the small area, and she looked up to find a girl watching her with wide eyes.

"Your Highness, forgive me." The girl bowed, lowering her gaze just like the other young woman had done.

Did everyone think she was a princess?

"No, I'm sorry. I shouldn't have barged in here." Mia let go of the curtain.

The girl looked at her again but didn't say anything else. Mia stepped into the booth and glanced over at the tables. Jewelry graced the surfaces, and Mia had to get a closer look. "These are beautiful." She ran her fingers over the smooth stones.

The young lady's face flushed at the praise. "Thank you, your Highness."

"Did you make this?" Mia lifted the bracelet and, sure enough, each stone wrapped around the wire.

"Of course, your Highness."

"Please, call me Mia."

The girl's eyes widened with a look of doubt or confusion as she fumbled over her words. "I couldn't do that ... Your Highness. It wouldn't be right."

"Check all the booths. She has to be here." The woman from the chapel called out from the street. What was Mia going to do now? They would no doubt find her, and there was nothing she could do to hide herself. She wasn't exactly dressed like the rest of the townspeople.

She set the bracelet down and searched around the booth for some way out. But would it really be so bad to go along with it for now? Just until she could figure out where she was? Mia didn't know anyone and had no money or identification with her. If she managed to escape, where would she sleep? And how would she eat until she could make it back to June?

The curtain swept open, and the woman's worried expression relaxed when her gaze landed on Mia.

"Princess Amelia, what are you doing?"

A knot of guilt formed in her stomach. She hesitated too long, and now she was out of options. This woman wasn't going to believe her anyway. She had to play along for now. "I was admiring this beautiful jewelry."

The woman sighed. "I was going to bring you to the festival tomorrow, your Highness." She gave a smile to the young woman. "I'm sure Luna would love to show you more of her designs after you're settled."

The girl beamed. "I would be honored."

"Great! Now, let's get you cleaned up and ready for your party." The woman held Mia's arm so she could slip on her shoes, then led her out of the booth and toward a waiting car.

A man in a uniform opened the back door, and Mia slid into the seat despite her high heels and long silk dress. The woman walked around the car and got in beside her.

"You said something about a party?"

The lady placed her clipboard on her lap and sighed. "Your engagement party to Prince Liam, of course. You must be so excited."

Mia's pulse skyrocketed. Wait. No one said anything about marriage. She reached for the door, scrambling to find the handle, but the car took off, leaving the booth and the sad, dreary court square behind.

Chapter Two

"Are you nervous?"

If those words had come from anyone other than Prince Liam Dunne's most trusted servant, he would quickly remind them who they were speaking to. Instead, he let out a long breath, ignoring the pit forming in his stomach, and answered the question. "Not really."

"You don't have to pretend with me, Your Highness."

Pretend? Perhaps Liam's perfectly crafted mask wasn't holding up as well as it should. A lifetime of keeping his emotions and facial expressions in check should have been enough to make him appear unbothered by today's events. "It's my duty to the United States Southern Sector."

The fact was, though, Liam should be nervous. He had agreed to an engagement with a complete stranger. He should be questioning everything and everyone who had a hand in this alliance.

But it wasn't his place to question. Not when his people needed him.

Instead, he stood still as his attendant adjusted his tie and hoped he could convince his parents and bride-to-be that he was content with this engagement.

"It is." Luka took a step backward and dropped his hands, but his gaze never left Liam's face.

"Why do I have the feeling there's a 'but' coming?"

A grin lifted the corners of Luka's mouth. "Just promise me you are doing this for the right reasons and not out of a sense of duty."

Okay, so he *had* to do better to mask his emotions. Or perhaps Luka just knew him better than most. Liam worked to clear the lump lodging in his throat. "I'm afraid duty is all I'm afforded."

Luka sighed, reaching for the navy suit jacket and holding it open for Liam to slide his arm through. "Surely, your parents would listen if you had someone else in mind, Your Highness."

Liam wanted to laugh out loud, but he bit the inside of his cheek instead. Even if someone else had caught his eye and claimed his heart, he wouldn't be able to follow his heart. His parents loved him, but not more than their people, property lines, and treaties. "I'm afraid, Luka, you'll just have to be disappointed. The only love I'm afforded is the one for my people."

A flash of pity flittered across his servant's face before it quickly vanished. "Well, if anyone could change their minds, it would be you, Your Highness."

Liam cleared his throat, stepped away from his attendant, and walked over to his desk. Pity wasn't what he wanted or needed. This was something he had to do—a necessity of his position. Everyone had a role to play in the Southern Sector. Since the Tenebrous Era.

Every aspect of society demanded and depended on it. The former US didn't climb out of destruction and rebuild for their monarchs to pick and choose which laws they abide by. If Liam could choose for himself this one time ... No, he couldn't think like that.

The intercom buzzed on his desk, and he eagerly pushed the button to answer it. Anything to distract his wayward thoughts. "Yes?"

"Your Royal Highness, Mr. Aspen is here to see you."

Liam looked at Luka in surprise. His servant merely shrugged. Liam shifted his attention back toward the intercom. "Thank you. Please send him in." What did his father's advisor want with him?

Mr. Aspen entered the office and bowed. "Your Highness."

"Mr. Aspen. What can I do for you?"

The man raised his head, and a frown played with the corners of his mouth. "Everything for a perfect summer engagement party is ready, and I was just alerted that Princess Amelia has finally arrived."

"That's great news, except the face you're making doesn't quite match your words."

Mr. Aspen's face turned bright red before he held up a tablet —one of the few in existence in the Southern Sector—from his side. "Well, it seems Princess Amelia arrived alone."

"What do you mean?"

"The royal engagement coordinator, Mrs. Bex, found her in the old chapel with no servants, attendants, or luggage." Mr. Aspen's voice grew more incredulous with each item he listed.

The old chapel? No one ever went to the abandoned chapel nestled just outside the town square. Not since official church services were outlawed after the Tenebrous Era. What happened, and why would she go there, of all places? "Is she all right?"

"She appears to be, Your Highness. They found her already dressed for the engagement party, but she was alone."

Liam raised an eyebrow at Mr. Aspen's reply. "And you are certain no entourage was with her?"

"None, sir."

His mind whirled in a hundred different directions. Princess Amelia would travel nowhere without guards and all her attendants—a caravan of vehicles and luggage.

What had happened? They must have run into some type of trouble on the road.

"Has there been any word from the Western Sector?"

Mr. Aspen tapped on the screen, and an exasperated sigh followed. "Well, considering this tablet is almost ancient, who knows if a message would get through even if they sent it."

A laugh tried to work its way through Liam's lips, but he held it at bay. "Oh, Mr. Aspen, you should be happy that our sector even has that tablet."

"Of course, Your Highness." If it were possible, the advisor's face turned a darker shade of red. The man did not like being called out, especially by Liam. Another couple of swipes on the screen, and he sighed. "No official word from the Western Sector, sir."

"All right. I'm sure she wouldn't have come alone, so something must have happened on her trip." He turned to Luka, a plan already forming in his mind. "Princess Amelia will need attendants."

"Of course, Your Highness. I will see to it myself."

Liam held up his hand. "Wait just a moment, Luka, before you go." He moved from his desk and gestured to Mr. Aspen. "Was there anything else that you needed, Mr. Aspen?"

The man raised his chin. "Well, perhaps we should send the advisor from the Western Sector in to welcome her."

Liam nodded and silently kicked himself. He should have thought of that and already had the man called for. If something happened on her trip, no doubt Princess Amelia would want and need to let her advisor know. The man had arrived several weeks ago on behalf of the Western Sector to plan and ready everything for his Princess's arrival. He was condescending and carried himself arrogantly, and for a moment, Liam wondered if he should even bother to send the man. No doubt the princess would be tired and possibly stressed, and Mr. Ortega wasn't exactly a comforting soul.

But for all he knew, Princess Amelia might be just like him. His stomach churned at the thought. Could he put up with someone who was the exact opposite of him for his entire life?

He longed to get out of this engagement. But he was already

committed, whether he wanted to be or not. And since he was, he couldn't fathom the idea of the woman being upset and scared.

"Yes, alert Mr. Ortega of her arrival and please send in my mother's maid to see to her until we can make other arrangements."

"Of course, Your Highness." Mr. Aspen bowed again before leaving the study.

Liam waited until the man was out of earshot before returning to Luka. Transfers between royal kingdoms didn't happen often—but Luka's family once served in the Western Sector. There were more affluent sectors, to be sure, but Liam had always been grateful that Luka had chosen the Southern Sector. Now, that decision could be an enormous relief to the princess.

"Luka, if Princess Amelia is alone, she's not going to feel very comfortable with the staff we have in the palace."

"That's probably true."

"Do you think your daughter would mind coming to the palace to help until Princess Amelia's attendants arrive?"

Luka's eyes widened, and he hesitated before he spoke. "She was a young girl when we made the trek here, Your Highness, and I'm not sure she would remember much about a servant's life at the palace."

"Well, perhaps just the knowledge she's from the princess's home sector would help." He sighed. "It may make the transition a little easier."

Luka nodded. "You are very kind to think about the princess like that."

"Well, I know firsthand how difficult this is." He sighed. "And I have my entire family and people here with me. She's all alone."

"I will talk to my daughter, Your Highness. I'm sure she would be happy to help."

"Thank you, Luka."

"It's no trouble. I will go ask her now." Luka bowed his head before departing, leaving Liam alone in the vast study.

He looked around, his eyes lingering on the clock in front of his desk. In two hours, his life would descend a path that, once started, could not be stopped. Liam did his best to ignore the dread filling his stomach and breaking his heart. He could do this.

Had to do this.

For his family, for the people, and for the Southern Sector.

Chapter Three

Mia's feet ached. Not only from those ridiculous high heels, but from pacing back and forth in some room. No—suite. *Her* suite. A *royal* suite.

A royal bedroom she didn't deserve or want. She wanted to celebrate at her sister's wedding reception, not to be stuck in a castle, pretending to be a princess—an engaged princess at that.

How did she go from her sister's wedding only hours ago to standing in a castle bedroom? How would she get out of this mess? Obviously, there was the truth. She should come clean and just tell them what happened. But each time someone entered the room, and she opened her mouth, she was at a loss for words.

Because what happened sounded more like a fairy tale than the actual truth. And who would believe her?

No one.

Because never in a million years would she believe such a story. If someone had approached her at her sister's wedding and said they were from another time, she would have them escorted out of the building.

And so would the lady who brought her to the castle. Or worse —would they throw her in a dungeon? A nervous laugh worked its way from her lips. *Ugh.* She was making herself crazy. Because who would believe that she fell through a window—a stained-glass window—that didn't even exist wherever it was she had landed?

No, her only course of action was to play along until she could come up with some sort of escape plan. Mia inhaled and exhaled slowly until her nerves calmed.

You can do this, Mia. You can pretend to be someone who you're not. She'd been in school plays, although she'd never had a speaking part. But still—how hard could it be?

She paused in front of a vanity mirror opposite a massive four-poster bed. The worried expression on her face caught her attention. *It would all be a lie.* Mia hated lying. And she was terrible at it. So, how was she supposed to pretend to be a princess?

Mia pulled the stool out and sat in front of the mirror. A crystal vase filled with a mixture of wildflowers graced the right side of the vanity—a simple but touching gesture.

One meant for a princess. An *engaged* princess. Pushing a tendril of hair behind her ear, Mia studied her reflection. Wide blue eyes, a nose just a tad too crooked, and not chubby, but round cheeks stared back at her. She didn't consider herself a knockout by any means, but princess material?

Ha!

A rap on the door startled her out of her pondering, and she jumped up, banging her knee in the process and rocking the vase of flowers.

"Are you all right, Your Highness?"

Mia righted the vase and brought her hands down to her sides. "Yes, of course."

A young lady entered, her expression furrowed. The worried look melted away, but not before Mia noticed her glance at the flowers before averting her gaze. The girl curtsied, then smiled.

"It's nice to see you again, Princess Amelia."

Again? Mia shuffled back through her very limited conversations since arriving at the palace before a flash of jewelry came to her mind. The girl in the market. "You're the jewelry maker from this morning?"

"Yes, Your Highness." The girl wheeled several cases into the room and shut the door. "I'm Luna, and I was asked to be your attendant until your servants arrive."

Her words held nothing but respect, but her tone almost begged for an answer. An explanation Mia did not know how to give or had time to even think of. Of course, a princess would arrive with help, and she was all alone.

"Oh. That's so very kind of you, Luna. But I couldn't expect you to leave your shop."

The girl's face flushed. "Prince Liam requested I serve you."

Great. Now, she'd just insulted the poor girl. Mia plastered on what she hoped was a sincere smile and one that appeared to understand the girl's reasoning. "Oh, I see."

"On accord that I'm also from the Western Sector." The girl raised an eyebrow. "So you would feel more comfortable."

Western Sector? What was this girl talking about? Wherever it was, it must be where this Princess Amelia was from. Mia cleared her throat. "Of course. Forgive me, Luna. I didn't realize you were from there as well."

The girl's eyes brightened. "That's all right, Your Highness. We left the Western Sector when I was a child, and it's been a while since I've been in the palace, but I have some memories of how things work."

Goosebumps rose on her arms as the maid's words sank in. Was that a warning? Did the girl already suspect that she was a fake?

Her shoulders tensed, and she straightened her back, trying to stand a little taller. If that was the case, and the girl was on to her, wouldn't she have sold her out this morning to the Engagement Coordinator lady? And if not, surely she would have once she was beckoned to the castle.

Whatever the case, Mia wanted to flee from the servant's

scrutinizing gaze but instead cleared her throat and gestured to the cart. "What do you have in there?"

"Oh!" The girl beamed. "The queen's maid found a few dresses and essentials that the queen had grown tired of. I believe they should all fit. If not, we can adjust them until we can get new garments made for you."

"Thank you, Luna. That's so very kind of you."

"I'll get you all unpacked."

"I can help."

The girl's hand froze on the case's zipper. "That's unnecessary, Your Highness."

"Please, Luna." Unbidden tears pricked her eyes. She needed something to take her mind off of everything. "I'm extremely nervous, and I would appreciate the distraction."

The servant studied her for a moment before finally sighing. "Just please don't tell anyone I made you help me."

Uh-oh. She didn't think such a tiny request could reflect poorly on the maid. The last thing she wanted was to cause trouble for Luna. "Of course not."

Luna handed gown after gown to Mia to place into the fancy wardrobe that matched the vanity and bed. Silk, velvet, and tulle tickled her fingers, and she had to refrain from running her hand across each and every dress. She had never seen anything like them. Each design was made for a queen, but each shade mimicked the ones she saw in the square earlier. Different varieties of blue, green, and gray, but almost dim, somehow. No bright and vibrant hues were among them. Nothing like her lavender bridesmaid dress. What would people think when they saw her? Was her dress too fancy for this Western Sector?

When Mia didn't think the wardrobe could possibly hold anything else, Luna pulled out corsets, slips, and stockings to fill the drawers of a nearby dresser. Then, they made quick work of filling the vanity with makeup and hair supplies.

"Look at the shoes!" Mia couldn't hide her excitement at

finding all the flats and ballet-type slippers in the bottom of the trunk. Thankfully, there weren't any heels.

"I'm sorry, Your Highness, but here in the Southern Sector, women do not often wear heels." The girl's eyes flickered to the silver heels that Mia kicked off as soon as she entered the bedroom.

"I can assure you, Luna, that will be a welcome change." Mia helped stack the shoes in the bottom of the wardrobe and tucked the knowledge that she was in the Southern Sector to think about later.

"You're all unpacked, and your hair still looks great from your trip. I believe you are ready for your Engagement Party."

The power of a full bottle of hair spray and a gifted hairdresser. Mia stood and walked over to where she discarded her shoes earlier. Her hands shook as her heart rate picked up its pace.

Was there a way she could get out of this Engagement party? Perhaps she could feign some type of sickness? It wouldn't be such a far-fetched excuse, given the fact she arrived alone. But that would bring up a whole slew of issues. Including questions about what happened to her, and she hadn't had the time to come up with a plan yet.

Could she just refuse to leave her room?

"Your Highness?"

Concern lined Luna's tone, which only heightened Mia's anxiety, bringing on a new wave of tears to form in the corners of her eyes.

The tension in her shoulders intensified, and a dull ache worked its way up her neck and settled behind her eyes. She would never pull this off, especially with a migraine setting in.

She had to at least make it a few days—to buy some time to come up with a plan. There had to be a way to get back home. Mia just had to find it. She could fake an engagement for a few days.

Right?

"I'm fine. I was just thinking I wouldn't mind trying a pair of those new shoes for the party."

A smile spread across Luna's face as she reached into the wardrobe and handed Mia a pair of gray flats. "How about these, Your Highness?"

"Perfect. If they will fit." They slid on with ease, and Mia bit back a smile. One minor obstacle out of the way—only a few hundred more to go.

Chapter Four

The news of the princess's arrival had the entire castle in an upheaval. She had never seen it quite like this. Luna bypassed several servants standing in a small group, whispering until they saw her and the princess start down the hallway. They stopped talking as they came closer. She stole a quick glance at Princess Amelia, but the princess was looking straight ahead.

If the ceased whispering and stares bothered Princess Amelia, she didn't let it show, which confirmed Luna's first impressions of the young woman. She was independent and determined—characteristics she desperately needed to flourish in the Southern Sector.

Luna should know. It wasn't often that a young woman owned a small business in the market square, either. But she did. And Luna had received her fair share of stares and whispers.

But even beneath the independence and determination, something else that Luna couldn't quite identify. Fear? Nervousness? She couldn't blame the princess for that. Traveling across the country to a new place where she didn't know a single soul? Terrifying.

She'd be nervous too. Another group of servants farther down the hall stopped to watch them, and this time, Luna couldn't bite her tongue.

"Don't you have someplace to be?" Luna hissed as she passed. They gasped at her sharp words, surprise registering in their eyes. Thankfully, though, they didn't say anything back as they scurried off. They had definitely recognized her from her time growing up in the palace.

She smoothed the fresh apron on the new-to-her servant's dress. The dark blue wool scratched her legs as she walked, and she clenched her fists to avoid the temptation to scratch.

Princess Amelia stopped directly behind her, eyes wide and hands clasped in front. As protocol dictated, Luna rapped on the door, then stepped backward so the princess would be in front.

They didn't have to wait long before Luna's father opened the prince's door to his private study. His kind and gentle blue eyes sought hers, lighting up before he greeted the princess with a smile and a bow.

"Good afternoon, Princess Amelia."

Princess Amelia hesitantly bowed her head in return, then flushed a bright red. "Good afternoon."

Luna's father opened the door wider and ushered them in, raising a fluffy eyebrow in her direction once the princess walked through. Reaching out, she squeezed his forearm and gave a brief shrug of her shoulders. So far, Princess Amelia wasn't like any royalty she'd encountered.

A gasp released from Luna's lips as she entered the study. She'd never been to this part of the castle before, and she had to reign in her excitement and not gawk at the homey great room. Worn but comfortable couches graced the edges of the room, nestled between large bookcases. Soft blankets decorated the back of the seats, most likely crocheted by a local artist. She clasped her hands in front of her so she didn't reach out and run her fingers over the beckoning fabric.

"Thank you for meeting us here, Your Highness. Prince Liam

thought you might like to take a moment to meet in private before attending the engagement party."

"That is very thoughtful of him."

"He will be here any moment. He wanted to walk over with your Sector's advisor."

Princess Amelia's eyes widened in sheer fright, and she suddenly froze. If just mentioning this man brought that amount of fear, there must be a reason. Should Luna do something?

She cleared her throat and stepped forward, wrapping her hand around her father's arm and steering him away from Amelia. "Father, I think Princess Amelia is exhausted from her trip, and perhaps it would be best for her nerves to just meet the prince right now. I'm sure Mr. Ortega would understand and meet with her later."

Her father looked over her shoulder to observe the princess, nodding as he took in her words. "*Ah*, well, if you think that's a good idea, then I'm sure Prince Liam wouldn't object, either."

"Thank you, Father. Why don't you wait outside and head them off?"

"Very well." He squeezed her hand and then bowed once more to the princess. "Please excuse me, Your Highness."

Amelia smiled and nodded, her back ramrod straight until he was out the door.

"Thank you so much, Luna." She rubbed her forehead. "I'm not feeling very well."

"It's no trouble, Your Highness." Luna frowned, taking a closer inspection of the princess. A sheen of sweat drenched her hairline, and her face paled with each passing second. "I'm sure everything will be all right."

"I'm not so sure."

Luna wanted to comfort the poor woman, but it would be improper. She wasn't a lady's maid or a servant. She was a merchant playing the part, and neither station afforded her the familiarity of comforting the princess. But Luna had never been able to bear to see anyone hurt. It was a blessing and a curse.

She would often see someone crying only to end up joining them. And Princess Amelia wasn't any different just because she was royalty. Before she thought better of it, Luna crossed the room and gently took the princess's hands. She gripped Luna's hands in response.

"Take a deep breath in, then let it out slowly."

Amelia's eyes filled, but she nodded and joined Luna in the breathing exercise.

"That's it." Luna gave her a reassuring smile. "Deep breath and let it out."

After a few moments, a bit of color flowed back into Amelia's cheeks. "Thank you, Luna. I don't know what came over me or what I would do if you hadn't intervened."

"You have a lot going on, and anyone would understand. Coming to a new place and the engagement."

Amelia sighed. "Yes, it is a lot all at once and just sort of hit me."

"It would anyone."

Voices outside the door interrupted their conversation. Luna dropped the princess's hands and took her place off to the side.

"Don't forget to breathe, Your Highness," Luna whispered as the double doors opened to the study. Prince Liam walked through, the advisor following close on his heels.

Chapter Five

Prince Liam nearly stopped in the doorway of his study and slammed the door in Princess Amelia's advisor's face. And it would serve him right. The man had been insufferable the entire time he awaited his princess's arrival, and now that she was here, he refused to let her have a few moments to gather her thoughts before he bombarded her with questions.

Questions that didn't need to be asked moments before she met her fiancé for the first time.

Liam didn't know what he expected when he laid eyes on the princess, but somehow it wasn't the sweet and nervous girl standing before him. She gripped the edges of her silk gown—a light and shimmery fabric they did not have here in the Southern Sector—something only the Western Sector could afford.

He hoped she wouldn't be too disappointed when she couldn't get that type of material shipped.

She stared at him with wide, blue eyes, full of caution. She seemed wary of him just as he was of her. Perhaps she was thinking about how poor and shabby he looked compared to everything she had at her fingertips.

And yet, he couldn't blame her for her caution. They were

complete strangers—two strangers who, in a few moments, would start a whole new life together.

Her rosy cheeks flamed darker the longer he stood there, letting the awkwardness linger between them. The last thing he wanted was for her to feel like he was judging her, so he cleared his throat and finally bowed in her direction. Something he should have immediately done. "Welcome, Princess Amelia."

The girl hesitated, then clumsily curtsied. "Thank you, Your Highness."

"Unhand me at once!"

Liam turned just in time to catch a glimpse of his servant, Luka, ushering two guards to the door to drag away an upset Mr. Ortega. Relief flooded him, knowing that Luka did what needed to be done without a direct order. He turned back to the princess.

"Looks like your advisor will have to give you a few moments now."

Relief filled the princess's eyes, and Liam knew he had made the right decision to listen to Luna's suggestion. Her hands let go of the fabric of her dress, her shoulders visibly relaxing along with the gesture.

He stepped toward her, trying to diffuse the situation's awkwardness. "I'd hoped we would get a chance to talk before the party tonight, but I'm afraid we are late getting to the banquet hall."

"Perhaps we can find more time this evening."

It was more of a statement than a question—one that made Liam chuckle. "You mean find time between the royal announcement, dance, feast, and pictures?"

Her face flushed crimson again, and she lowered her eyes. "You can't talk while dancing or enjoying your dinner, Your Highness?"

The princess glanced up at him, a small smile playing in the corners of her mouth. Perhaps they could find some common ground after all. If she could tease him, then he would enjoy giving it right back. He closed the distance between them and offered his arm. "Do you actually suggest we should enjoy ourselves tonight?"

She hesitated for a moment before wrapping her arm through his, her icy fingers seeping through his thin shirt sleeve. "Well, it is our party, after all."

"Indeed, it is." Liam gently ushered her out of the room, thankful that Luka made sure Mr. Ortega was nowhere in sight to bombard them.

He guided her down the passageways of his private rooms, back into the main stairwell that led to the public banquet hall.

Amelia kept a firm grip on his arm, her gaze never leaving the hallway. If he were in her shoes—coming to live in the Western Sector—he would no doubt try to take in everything around him. "Are you all right?" he whispered, in case any of the servants following behind them were listening.

"I'm—fine."

He stopped and covered her hand on his arm with his free one. The sudden urge to acknowledge their situation and where he was coming from hit him. "I'm not even going to pretend that what we are doing is easy because it's not. We don't know each other, and we certainly don't love each other."

She opened her mouth to reply, but he hurried on. "But I do know that I hope you will find some happiness here." He already blurted out the cold, hard truth. He might as well keep going. "It's my hope that we could at least have a friendship."

"A friend sounds really nice right about now." Her voice cracked on the words, and she looked away.

Carefully, he reached over and gently touched her chin, turning it back toward him. Tears dampened the corner of her eyes. What an unfair situation for both of them. He was forced to give up the opportunity to one day find love. But so was she, and now that she was here, standing inches away, he wanted to give her something. Anything to take the pain away. "I promise that from here on out, you will always be able to depend on me."

He meant to promise she could depend on his friendship, but

the words were out, and he didn't amend them. Maybe it was how she looked up at him—as if she needed to hear those words so much that he promised more than he intended. But he kept his mouth closed, waiting for her to say something in return.

She turned, reaching out to hold onto his other arm as well. "Prince Liam, there's something that I have to tell you right now before—"

The doors to the ballroom pulled open, and Liam broke her hold, gently guiding her back to his side and extending his arm for her to hold once more. "You'll have to tell me later, Princess." He stole a glance and winked at her. "Perhaps while we are dancing."

Chapter Six

A few sweet words and one promise from a handsome prince, and Mia was about to confess she wasn't the real princess?

What was wrong with her?

But when he stared at her with those warm, honey-colored eyes, declaring a promise bound in honor, duty, and kindness, she wanted to confess the truth to him. And she would have had the doors not opened, breaking the spell and centering her right back into reality.

Back to Plan *A*. All she had to do was get through this engagement party, and then she could get out of there and return home. Simple enough.

But first, she had to make it through this party.

Hard to do when hundreds of people surrounded them, dressed in finery and beaming in their direction. Vases of flowers on tall pedestals decked out the room, and she focused on the nearest bouquet of roses instead of the crowd's attention.

"People of the Southern Sector, I'm pleased to announce His Royal Highness, Prince Liam Dunne, and Her Royal Highness, Princess Amelia Lockridge."

So, Lockridge was her last name? Mia added that to her

running list of details she was collecting and scanned the crowd for the announcer. Finally, she found him standing not too far away from what must be Liam's parents. Panic tried to overwhelm her again, and she gripped Liam's arm. He tensed for a moment, then covered her hand with his. His touch was warm, and his thumb rubbed the back of her hand as he gently led her through the crowd. Attendants bowed as they passed.

He leaned toward her and whispered, "You're doing great."

"I'm glad you think so." She matched his tone and mentally gave herself a shake. She had to get her act together. A Princess would never let her emotions get the best of her. She would have practiced standing regal and tall her whole life before her people. Not having fits of nervousness and panic.

Except, these weren't her people. She didn't have a lifetime of experience, and she wasn't a real princess.

And while she was being honest, anxiety liked to rear its ugly head during stressful moments. Right now, she'd never been more stressed in her entire life. Instead of letting her thoughts get the best of her and clutching Liam's arm, she forced her fingers one by one to relax.

The prince led her past his parents toward the middle of the ballroom floor. He dropped her arm and turned to face her, bowing from his waist. What was he doing? *Ugh.* She was so bad at curtsying. She'd done it a few times and almost fell over each time. Now, she would fall flat on her face in front of hundreds of people.

Liam raised his head slowly, his amber eyes twinkling even though his face was void of emotion as if he expected her to curtsy awkwardly. Letting out a deep breath, she did her best to keep her body straight but elegant as she bowed. There weren't any gasps or titters of laughter, so she must have done all right. The prince gently grabbed her waist, pulling her closer as violins played to their right.

Finally, something that she wasn't terrible at or had to fake. She placed her hand on his arm and the other in his hand. June had insisted she come to dance lessons with her before the wedding, and now it looked like her sister's bossiness would pay off.

After a few turns around the floor, other couples joined them, and Mia relaxed, knowing that not every pair of eyes was fixated on her.

"You're not talking."

Mia nearly stumbled at Liam's voice, low and breathless in her ear, but righted herself quickly enough. "What?"

"You said dancing was the perfect time to talk." He lifted their arms and spun her, that twinkle in his eyes back again.

"Did I?" Mia laughed breathlessly as she twirled. "Maybe I overestimated my ability to carry on a conversation and keep up with your fancy footwork."

"*Ah.*" Liam spun her out, bringing her back in inches from his face. "I should have been a gentleman and started the conversation. But I've been distracted."

A smile lifted the edges of his mouth, lighting up his face. The corners of his eyes wrinkled when he grinned, distracting Mia from everyone else around them. His gaze lowered to her lips, and she ceased to even hear the music playing anymore or notice the couples spinning around them.

"How so?"

"By trying to make sure you stay upright."

Mia leaned back, the magic of the moment gone, except Liam started laughing, and she joined in. "So, I compliment your fancy footwork, and you call me clumsy." Liam spun her back around into a normal dancing position.

"What can I say? You seem to bring out my funny side."

"So, is this what I have to look forward to? Endless teasing?"

"I wouldn't call it *endless*. I'm not cruel."

"Well, sir, two can play at that game." Mia flashed him a smile just as the song came to a finish. She clapped with the other guests, sneaking a couple of glances at Liam. His servant, she couldn't remember his name, appeared at their side, but she couldn't make out his words over the crowd or the band, which had started another song.

After a moment, Liam held out his arm for her. "It's time for the photos and then dinner."

"Photos after we've been dancing?" Mia reached up and quickly checked her hair, which was somehow still secured.

"You look beautiful." Liam grinned and then added. "Although it sounds a little silly, now that you bring it up." He motioned for his servant. "Please have Luna meet us in the gardens with whatever Princess Amelia may need for the photos."

"Of course, Your Highness."

The crowd continued to dance around them as Mia followed Liam off the dance floor and to the back of the ballroom. A servant standing by the entrance opened the door for them, and Mia sucked in a deep breath as she stepped out into a garden patio.

Twinkling white lights were hung along the trees surrounding the patio's border. The area was beautiful but not overdone, which seemed to be a running theme at the castle. Fine fabrics but muted in hues. Nice architecture but modest. Fine dishes and decorations, but not gaudy. It seemed the royal family appreciated the finer things of life but didn't flaunt it to their people.

It was refreshing, yet she did not know how she could possibly fit in. This engagement photo would be the proof.

She rubbed the back of her neck, trying to erase the tension. The headache from earlier would be a full-blown migraine before long. Did they even have headache medication?

"Excuse me, Your Highness, I thought you might want this." Luna held out her bouquet from June's wedding. "They are so beautiful."

"Thank you, Luna." Her voice wavered as she reached for the flowers. "They will look lovely."

"Are you all right?"

"Of course." Mia grasped the flowers and noticed Luna's forearm was bright red. "Luna, whatever happened?"

"Oh, it's nothing." Luna pulled down the sleeve of her shirt.

"That's *not* nothing."

Luna ignored her, plastering on a fake smile. "Let's tuck a few of those stray strands of hair back into place."

"Luna, you can trust me." Mia didn't know if she would have any reason to believe her, but she couldn't stand the idea of someone hurting the poor girl. "If someone is hurting you—"

Luna's eyes widened in surprise. "Princess Amelia, you mustn't worry. I'm fine. Now, you have a prince waiting for you." She gestured toward Liam, who was already in place under a canopy of ivy and clear lights.

There had to be more to this story, but Luna's words held a level of pleading under them. She didn't want to discuss it and now wasn't the time or place.

Mia gripped the bouquet in her sweaty hands and crossed over to the patio to join Liam. The photographer placed them side by side and snapped a few pictures before prompting Liam to wrap his arm around her waist. With each flash of the camera, the pounding of her head intensified.

How did Mia go from dreading posing for her sister's wedding photographs to standing next to a royal prince for her engagement?

Chapter Seven

The soothing mixture of orange and pink of the rising sun did nothing to slow Luna's racing thoughts. After a fitful night of sleep, she finally gave up and dressed, wishing she'd agreed to stay in her father's small apartment in the castle instead of the tiny servant's room near the royal floor. There, she could have at least had the comfort of knowing her dad was nearby. Instead, she teased him that she would get more sleep without hearing his loud snoring.

Living quarters for the maids and lady's maids were once with the other castle servants, near the kitchen but far from the royal bedrooms. In an effort to become more efficient, the maids' quarters were moved a floor away from the royal family suites. While the other servants seemed thrilled with their new living situation, Luna longed for the humble two-room loft in the merchant's square above her jewelry shop. She would take her chipped painted walls and worn floor covered in blue rugs over this refurbished supply room.

The shelves for linens still occupied the left wall, with a bed and dresser taking up the other two. The only advantage of this room was that it had a window. One that opened. Well, after Luna spent nearly twenty minutes prying it open.

Would it be too early to check on Princess Amelia? Luna's hand froze on the window latch. Who was this imposter? And why was this girl pretending to be the princess of the Western Sector?

She gingerly rubbed the fingerprint bruises on her forearm. They were sore and turning a lovely shade of purple. After they arrived at the ballroom last night, Mr. Ortega grabbed her arm and yanked her back into the hallway and into an empty room. When she tried to get away, he threw her against the wall and pinned her there, demanding that she play along that the young woman was the true princess, even though she knew Princess Amelia was an imposter.

Stunned, Luna didn't know what to do or say, so she nodded in shock as the man threatened her and her father if she didn't comply.

It took several moments to peel herself from the wall and return her heart rate to normal. She wasn't afforded the luxury of having time to process her thoughts or what had happened. She still had a job to do, and her absence wouldn't go unnoticed.

Now, last night's events were all she could think about. Inhaling the crisp morning air, she closed her eyes and enjoyed the breeze on her face before pulling away and shutting the window. With a quick tug, she pulled down the sleeves of her uniform, which would hide most of the bruises. But it wouldn't stop the princess from noticing. This imposter was too observant.

It took Amelia all of ten seconds to spy the redness on her arm moments after she reappeared at her side just in time for the pictures. Part of her wanted to stop thinking of her as the princess —but she couldn't forget Mr. Ortega's menacing and evil sneer as he threatened her father.

Even if she wanted to out the princess, she didn't think she could. Luna didn't know much about the young woman, but something about her drew Luna to her and made her want to protect her—to know her more—to befriend her.

Besides, anyone who showed that much compassion for a

maid automatically earned respect in Luna's eyes.

Bells from the grandfather clock in the hallway chimed six long trills. Still early, but it wouldn't be long before the other servants were up and readying the royal family for breakfast. She took her time sliding on her shoes, fixing her hair, and shaking out the wrinkles on her apron.

When she couldn't stall any longer, she slipped out her bedroom door and into the dark hallway, finding the light switch and flipping it on. The hum of electricity filled the space before the light turned on, its dim light barely illuminating the floor. Luna was amazed that electricity wasn't used to its full capabilities even in the palace.

Rounding the last corner before the stairwell, Luna reached for the switch to flip the light back off as they were told to do when exiting the servant's quarters.

"Have you made a decision?"

"Mr. Ortega!"

The menacing voice of the Western Sector's advisor called out of the stairwell's shadows. He stepped forward, blocking the entrance. Her body recoiled at the sight of him, but she couldn't get her feet to move.

"Come on, girl. I don't have all day."

Finally, she stepped backward, distancing herself from the man and his angry words. Her voice wavered, but she managed to reply. "Mr. Ortega, I'm just a maid. It's not my place to do anything."

"You expect me to believe that?" He challenged, his lips turning into a scowl. "You're Luka's daughter."

Swallowing hard, she nodded and tried to hide her fear. There was something cruel and violent in the man's eyes. "As you said, sir. We are just servants."

"Don't play games with me, girl." Mr. Ortega grabbed her bruised arm, and she cried out in pain.

"Please, Mr. Ortega, I don't understand what you want from me."

"Your father has the prince's ear. He would believe anything you or your father says. And I need everyone to believe that she is, in fact, the princess."

Luna tried to rip her arm away from the man, but he yanked, pulling her uncomfortably close, his rank breath turning her stomach. "Now, you're going to play along. You will teach that girl everything she needs to play the part of Princess Amelia, and you will keep your mouth shut."

"I don't even know Princess Amelia—"

"But you're from the Western Sector. You know the customs."

She might have been from the Western Sector, but she was just a little girl when they left. "Mr. Ortega, I don't remember much about our life there."

"Well, you better figure it out. You're the only one who can pull this off." He looked down at her, his lips curling into a cruel smile. "And if you don't, I will let it be known that your father still worships the God from before the Tenebrous Era."

Luna forgot how to breathe.

He wouldn't do that.

She started to answer, but the look in his eyes stopped her, and Luna had to look away.

"*Ah*, now you're getting it." He shoved her backward once more, her head hitting the wall. "Now, do we have a deal or not?"

Scenarios of her father's imprisonment, banishment, or worse —death—played out in her mind. Each one was more horrific than the one before. What else could she do?

"Answer me!" He pulled her forward and rammed her again into the wall. A wave of dizziness washed over her, and she barely got the words out. "You have ... you have a ... deal."

"Good girl." He released her, stood back, and adjusted his suit. "We'll talk again soon."

Luna somehow managed to keep her tears at bay until he left her, his footsteps echoing down the staircase. When they finally faded, she slumped down to the floor and sobbed.

Chapter Eight

Liam pushed his chair back from the dining room table and stood, waiting for his parents to take their places at the table. "Good morning."

"Good morning, my dear." His mother embraced him before claiming her seat across from him. "Where's your betrothed?"

"She hasn't made an appearance yet." Liam sat and placed his napkin across his lap.

"Do they not eat breakfast in the Western Sector?" Father grunted, waving over the servants. In seconds, they lifted trays of biscuits, ham, and fruit and placed them in the center of the table.

"I'm sure they do, Father." Liam reached for the glass of freshly squeezed orange juice. "Princess Amelia seemed to have a headache last night. She may still be resting."

"Poor thing." Mother shook her head. "After her long journey, she deserves the rest. Let's eat. No reason for this wonderful feast to get cold."

Liam met his mother's eyes and gave her a smile. She returned the grin, but neither one reached for their forks. As a child, Liam thought it was a game his mother played with him, but as he grew up, he learned just how important it was. He silently prayed a blessing over his food—with his eyes open—just like his mother had taught him.

Seconds later, his mother grabbed her fork, and he followed suit. His father had already begun eating, not paying a bit of attention to them. Whether his father knew that his wife and son were believers and chose to overlook it, Liam didn't know.

"What do you have planned for this week's engagement activities?" Mother interrupted his thoughts, and he didn't realize that he had yet to take a bite of food. He quickly opened a biscuit and spread jelly across it.

"I thought I would take Princess Amelia to the court square today. Show her the artisan shops." He took a bite and set it back on his plate. "I'm still trying to decide for the rest of the week. I thought a picnic and perhaps seeing a play sounded fun."

His mother nodded in approval. "That sounds lovely." She turned to Father. "Harold, we haven't been to the theater in ages. Doesn't that sound like fun?"

His knife skidded across the plate at the interruption. "I don't understand why everyone insists on these activities between the engagement. There are four events. Isn't that enough?"

"Oh, Harold, seriously?" Mother frowned. "If I remember correctly, you planned several outings for our engagement."

"Scarlett, dear, I believe you planned everything."

"No, I didn't. I remember it was your idea to take a boat out on the lake to star gaze."

Liam nearly choked on a piece of ham. "Father, you took Mother out on the lake at night to look at the stars? I didn't know you were so romantic."

"*Ha!* It was far from romantic when we were surrounded by security and chaperones."

Mother grinned. "It was the thought that counted."

Liam couldn't imagine trying to get to know someone with everyone listening in on their conversations. At least now, the security team blended in with the crowd and only came near when or if a threat was detected. He finished his breakfast and signaled the servant.

"Would you please bring me a clean plate?"

"Of course, Your Highness."

"I think I'm going to take a plate to Princess Amelia and make sure she's feeling okay."

"That's very sweet, Liam." Mother placed her napkin on the table. "I must get going as well. These roses aren't going to trim themselves."

"Scarlett, we have a gardener for that."

She laid a hand on Father's shoulder. "I know, dear, but it's good for the soul."

"If the courtiers see you doing that—"

"They'll what? Petition the king?" She leaned down and kissed the top of his head. "It's a good thing I know him."

"Will you at least let the gardener help you?"

Mother laughed. "Perhaps. Have a good day, Liam."

He nodded and filled a plate for Princess Amelia, unsure of her favorites, so he got a little of everything. "See you tonight, Father."

He mumbled a reply, but Liam was already out of the door and making his way up to the family's floor. Several servants passed on the way and asked if he needed assistance, eying the plate of food in one hand and a glass of juice in the other. No doubt, it was a sight to see. The prince acting as a servant.

At the top of the stairs, two guards moved out of the way, expecting him to turn to his family's wing, but instead, he went left, passing several guest rooms before arriving at the one assigned to Amelia.

He should have thought about this more thoroughly and brought the tray as well. He shifted the plate to balance on his arm and somehow held the juice without dropping either to knock on the door quickly.

Moments later, Amelia was at the door, pulling her robe

tighter around her. "Your Highness." Both hands went up to smooth her hair. "I wasn't expecting you."

"I'm sorry to bother you, Princess Amelia. I was just worried when you didn't come down for breakfast."

Her shoulders relaxed some, but Liam noticed her red and puffy eyes. She had been crying. "I overslept."

Concern instantly filled him. "Was it your headache? I noticed you seemed to be hurting last night."

Her cheeks reddened. "I couldn't sleep and spent most of the night awake."

"If your bed isn't suitable, I can move you to a more comfortable suite."

"The bed is fine, and the room is beautiful." She shrugged her shoulders. "I never sleep when I'm away from home."

"Oh, do you travel often?" Liam sighed. She would certainly be disappointed to learn that traveling within the Southern Sector was a luxury, not even the royal family did it often.

"Enough to know that I prefer my own bed." Her eyes widened, and she shook her head. "I'm sorry, that must sound so rude. I'm just missing—"

"Your home, I understand. You have nothing to apologize for." He looked at the floor and suddenly remembered the food. "I brought you some breakfast. I didn't know what you liked, so I just grabbed a variety."

She accepted the plate, a smile spreading across her face. "This looks amazing. Thank you."

"You're welcome." Why did he feel so nervous? He squashed down his unease. "I thought I could take you to the market square today if you'd like."

"I would love that."

"Great. Have Luna send word when you're ready to go."

"Sure." Her tone sounded anything but certain.

"Is something wrong?"

"How do I go about getting in touch with Luna?"

Liam wanted to laugh out loud but quickly banished the unbidden laughter. Her face was red again, and alerted to her embarrassment. They must have a different intercom system in the Western Sector. Of course, they would. They could afford the newest versions.

He pointed over her shoulder to the common room. "May I?"

"Oh, of course." She stepped back, placed the food in the sitting room, and ushered him in.

"Each room has an intercom box." He searched the room and found it on an end table beside the couch. "Here it is."

"I didn't even see that."

"Just push the button. The intercom will ring to the servant's area, and they will come to you. If you are in your suite, it will ring to Luna personally."

"And if I'm not in here?"

"They are all color-coded. Which, now that I think about it, you will need a color assigned. I'm sorry, we've never had a new family member join ..." He cleared his throat. "It's always just been my parents and myself."

"It's okay. You don't have to explain."

An uncomfortable silence filled the space between them before Liam finally got to his feet to move toward her door which he left open for propriety's sake. "I will have Luka assign you a color, and I will see you in a little while."

"Sounds like a plan."

He bowed slightly and backed out of the room, watching the door close. Could he be any more awkward? Granted, he'd never been engaged to someone before.

Get it together, Liam, before she completely backs out of this union.

Wouldn't that be a mess? He could only imagine what the courtiers, his parents—and the council—would say and do if this alliance fell through.

Too many people were counting on him to uphold his end of

the engagement. Since he couldn't find any other solution to the shipping problems the Southern Sector had endured the past few years, the engagement to Princess Amelia was the only answer.

And he couldn't do anything to mess it up.

One event down, three more to go.

Chapter Nine

There had to be a way to distract Prince Liam during the marketplace tour and return to the chapel. Of course, the glass wouldn't be there, but maybe it didn't have to be. Mia had read enough books and watched movies to know that sometimes these things worked in a time frame. Maybe it was simply a one-time-a-day thing.

You know how ridiculous you sound, right? This is not a work of fiction. It's your life.

Even if she could somehow get away from Liam, there was still the matter of Luna and her father, and no doubt the other guards mixed into the crowd.

"What do you think of our humble marketplace?"

Mia looked over at her walking companion with a genuine smile. "It's charming. I love watching people enjoy themselves."

He seemed to ponder her answer for a moment. "I suppose I never stopped to think about that before."

From what she had witnessed from the prince so far, his confession surprised her. He had been nothing but thoughtful about what she might need since she'd arrived. "Perhaps you just haven't had the chance to observe before. Do you come to the town square often?"

"I'm afraid not." He stopped and turned toward her. "I take it you do all of your shopping, then?"

Was this a trick question? Unease wafted over her. She just didn't know enough about life in this new time to answer without the chance of being found out. Perhaps if she answered his questions generically, she could get out of that scrutinizing gaze he turned on her when he asked her about her life.

"No, but I do enjoy shopping." It wasn't a total lie. June did most of the shopping for them.

Seeming somewhat satisfied, the prince started walking again, and Mia turned to find Luna a few steps away from them, watching the crowd. Every few seconds, she turned back to Mia. The entire time she helped Mia get ready, she was in a hurry and distant, like she didn't want to be there. Add in the fact that she tried to cover up swollen, puffy eyes, and Mia knew the poor girl was upset about something.

"Luna, is your shop nearby?"

Startled, the servant jumped at being addressed. "Oh! Yes, Your Highness. It's just a block away."

"May we go visit it? I would love to see your jewelry again."

"Of course, Your Highness." She fumbled over her words. "That is—if it's all right with Prince Liam."

The prince handed over a few coins at the booth they were stopped at and passed Mia a bouquet of wildflowers. "For you, Your Highness."

"They're beautiful." She accepted the flowers and inhaled the sweet fragrance. The flowers were a splash of happiness in a sea of muted blues and grays. "I asked Luna if we could visit her shop. Would it be all right if we head that way now?"

The prince's face brightened. "Of course. A little birdie told me you enjoyed the jewelry on your arrival."

Luckily, he didn't elaborate or press her for questions about that day. No one had bothered her with the details of her arrival, and the princess's advisor had not come to talk to her yet, which kept her at a constant level of nervousness. They would inevitably inquire, and she had to come up with some type of cover story.

Which would require more lies. Her heart picked up pace, and sweat beaded along her hairline. She hated to lie, but what else could she do? She was stuck in the future with nothing to her name.

"Here we go." Luna unlocked the door and pulled back the curtain for them to enter. It was just like Mia had seen it the other day, except now she could browse. She looked at each table, taking her time to appreciate the beauty of each piece. She could only imagine how long Luna would take to craft each one.

A small display case in the back caught Mia's eye. She made her way to the case and nearly squealed out loud. In two neat rows were bracelets, rings, and necklaces made of colorful stones.

Bright colors!

Shocked, Mia bent down to get a closer look. Some were on a silver chain, and some were wrapped with wire in intricate designs and knots. But on the far right was a silver bracelet with dainty diamond stones with a teal-colored jewel in the center.

"Would you like to see the bracelet, Your Highness?"

Mia looked up to find Luna behind the case, pulling out a key ring. "Yes, please."

Luna grinned, slipping the bracelet out of the case and gently laying it in her palm. Tiny sparkles glistened in the light.

"Do you like it?" Liam's voice appeared beside her, a smile on his face.

"It's gorgeous." Mia rubbed her thumb over the smooth stones. "Luna, you are so talented."

"You're too kind, Your Highness." Luna blushed, adverting her eyes from Mia. She didn't mean to embarrass the girl, but she had genuine talent, which shouldn't go unnoticed.

Prince Liam gestured to the bracelet. "Then you should have it."

"Oh, no, I couldn't." Mia shook her head. There was no telling how much something like this cost, and she didn't exactly have any money on her when she fell through the window. Not that she suspected her funds would work in this strange place. She started to hand it back to Luna, but Liam swept it up and pointed to her wrist.

"Please, Princess Amelia. Consider it a welcome gift." He grinned, his eyes wrinkling in the corners—a grin she was growing quickly to enjoy. "May I?"

She hesitated, unsure whether she should accept such a gift. But Liam looked so happy to offer, and how could she deny Luna the profit of such beautiful artwork? She held up her arm, and he clasped it around her wrist.

"Thank you, Your Highness."

"You're most welcome." He paid Luna and turned back to Mia. "What do you say we get some lunch and eat in the park?"

"I would like that."

Prince Liam led her down the street to a small café of sorts. The building was weather-worn, its siding sagging, and in need of a fresh coat of paint. But the line went out the door and down the block, so the food must be good.

"Where are you going?" Liam asked, reaching for her arm and gently pulling her to a stop.

"The line—the back is this way."

"Yes, well, there's another door for us to place our order."

"Oh." Mia frowned. One more thing she'd done wrong. Of course, a prince wouldn't stand in line with commoners.

As if sensing her frustration, Prince Liam added, "It's just a safety measure."

"I'm sorry. I wasn't thinking."

"There's nothing you need to apologize for." He offered her his arm, and they walked around the back of the store and up the stairs. "What are you in the mood for? The cook here makes incredible chicken and dumplings."

"You better believe I do!"

A curvy woman with red hair and a motherly smile poked her head out of the kitchen. "I thought I heard the prince's voice."

"I couldn't come to the marketplace and not taste the best chef's cooking in all the Southern Sector."

The woman laughed and pointed her finger at him. "You keep spreading that rumor, and now I can't keep up with the demand."

"If only you would return to the castle like we've been begging for years. You could have a whole kitchen staff to help you." Liam teased, embracing the woman in a hug.

"You know I can't leave all of these starving people." She leaned back, tears in the corners of her eyes. "But it blesses my heart to know you care."

"I wish I could do more."

"I know you're doing all you can." She grinned, gesturing to Mia. "Look at your gorgeous new fiancée."

"Oh, forgive my terrible manners." Liam reached for Mia's hand. "Princess Amelia, this is Mrs. Vera."

"It's a pleasure to meet you."

"Oh, the pleasure is all mine, Your Highness." Vera held her arms up. "I like to give hugs, so bring it in."

The woman enveloped Mia in a big embrace, and she nearly melted at the sudden flood of emotion. The older woman had a grandmotherly touch that Mia hadn't had since she was a young girl.

"She can get away with it since she helped raise me." Prince Liam leaned against the kitchen counter. "Mrs. Vera was my governess for a long time and then became the chef."

"Yes, I was." She beamed at the prince. "And when I moved to the kitchen, he followed."

"What do you mean?" Mia asked, enjoying the easy banter between the two.

"Well, this one here loves to sneak sweets. I would catch him sneaking down to the kitchen every day. Finally, I just put him to work. And he's turned out to be a right fine cook too."

"That's amazing. I've never been that great at cooking." Mia wrinkled her nose, remembering all the times June came home to burned dinners. "I would love to watch you make something."

"Sadly, our new chef doesn't like us to invade the kitchen."

"Well, you can come use mine anytime." Vera sighed. "Now, what can I get you two? I have a new pot of chicken and dumplings on the stove."

"That sounds amazing, Mrs. Vera."

"Two orders coming right up." She patted Liam's shoulder. "I'll even throw in some dessert."

"Perfect."

They were out of the café and in the park within ten minutes. It wasn't much of a park, though. There were trees and a small area of green grass, but that was about it. No landscaping, walking paths, or children's playground equipment. A few benches lined the outer perimeter, and several groups of young mothers sat while their kids dug in a dirt patch.

"Is something the matter?" Prince Liam put his spoon in his bowl. "I know all of that probably seemed odd to you."

"I think it's very sweet that you still keep in touch with your governess."

"Well, Mrs. Vera is a special lady. More like my grandmother."

"You're lucky."

"Why is that?"

Mia could kick herself. She needed to get a hold of her mouth. Was Princess Amelia's grandmother even still alive? "To have a grandmother still around."

His face softened. "I'm sorry. I didn't even think how that might make you homesick."

"It's all right." She took a bite of the dumplings and nearly groaned out loud. Prince Liam was correct. These were delicious. "May I ask you a question?"

"Of course."

"Why aren't there things for the children to play with?"

Liam wiped his mouth with a napkin and leaned back in his chair. "Well, the Southern Sector has long since taken a stance on humility and living well beneath the Sector's means since the Tenebrous Era."

"But surely a swing set or something simple like that isn't an extravagant expense."

Liam's tone shifted to a much darker cadence than she'd heard from him. "No, it's not, but it's not likely to happen either."

"I didn't mean to overstep—"

"You didn't, Princess Amelia. I wish I could make it happen. But some things are simply out of my control."

"That must be very hard. To see a need and not be able to fulfill it." There had to be something Mia could do to help brighten up the park. Plant flowers? Recycle items into some sort of play area?

"Your Highness, you're needed back at the castle."

Mia was so engrossed in her thoughts and Liam's sudden change in demeanor that she didn't even notice the servants who had appeared at their side.

Luka leaned closer to whisper more to Liam, but Mia thought she heard the words *shipment* and *uproar*.

Luna was already packing their food in a basket and walking it to the nearby car.

Liam stood from the bench and offered his hand. "I'm sorry, Princess Amelia, but we must head back."

"Is everything all right?"

Luka's worried expression told her it wasn't, but instead, he said, "It will be."

Chapter Ten

It was all he could do to mask his emotions on the car ride back to the palace. Princess Amelia didn't say much, no doubt feeling the tension radiating from him.

The outing to the marketplace went far better than Liam had envisioned, and he enjoyed the princess's company. He hated that he had to end it early.

A beautiful day for a picnic was cut short by an attack on the shipping convoy. He had been enjoying a wonderful meal while rebels were stealing from his people.

Again.

The thought made him sick to his stomach. He was the crowned prince of the Southern Sector. His father had entrusted him with the border treaties, shipments, and the council, and he was desperately failing them all.

He thought the first step would be his engagement to Princess Amelia. Then, he could focus on these rebels, who grew bolder with each attack.

Once they arrived at the palace and Liam parted ways with Amelia in the main hallway, he turned toward his personal study. He didn't have to look back to know his servant would be right on his heels.

He practically ran to his study, eager to get away so they could talk in private.

"What's the damage, Luka?"

"We don't know yet, Your Highness." He sighed, closing the door once they entered the study. "A new shipment of fruit and vegetables arrived today. It was unloaded successfully from the train, but as soon as they started to bring it to the warehouse, the rebels opened fire, sending the workers running for cover."

Liam couldn't find fault with the workers not defending the convoy. That wasn't part of their job description. "I don't understand this at all! Don't they realize that every shipment we receive is distributed to the marketplace? Only a small portion of the supplies go to the palace."

"There's a food shortage, Your Highness. And people are hungry and worried."

"But our people aren't attacking, Luka." He slammed his fist on his desk. "These rebels are the ones attacking. And we know next to nothing about them!"

Luka sighed. "The king has deployed a team to gather intelligence. It's only a matter of time before we know more."

"I'm afraid it will be too late." Liam collapsed in his chair. "The shipments are already too few and far between, and now we can't even hold on to what we do manage to get in."

"You must have faith, Liam."

"I do, Luka. But it's being overrun with fear at the moment."

Luka nodded and pulled out a chair in front of Liam's desk. He only did this when he wanted to have a conversation about the old ways. "Well, you know what I say when that happens."

Liam rubbed his forehead. The verse already popping into his mind. "We were not given a spirit of fear." He let out a deep and long breath. "I wish my father believed that. It would make talking to him about these matters so much easier."

"Your father has lost the way, Liam." His voice was soft and gentle. "Just like the generations before him. The Tenebrous Era brought a lot of devastation, but perhaps this is its most painful one."

Liam couldn't refute that. Having faith in God was not tolerated in the new US. Some Sectors were more lenient than others. Luka, his mother, himself … they all believed, at their own peril.

"We must have faith for them."

He wanted to roll his eyes, but he wouldn't disrespect his friend in such a manner. "You make it sound so simple."

"One day, you will be king."

Liam snorted. "That's hardly the answer, Luka."

"Isn't it?"

Having faith, he could do. Praying, he could do. Being the one to bring about change? That was entirely another beast to tame. "You want me to not only solve these shipment and border problems but also reverse the ban on faith?"

"You're marrying Princess Amelia, so you're halfway there." A teasing smile lifted Luka's lips. "But for now, focus on what you can do. Like dispersing what's left of the food."

He was right. The rebels might have made a dent in the food, but hopefully, something would be left. And they had the warehouse itself to think about. It wasn't where it should be, but it was something.

"Have the Captain of the Guard bring half of what the castle usually takes."

"Your father will not like that."

Liam shrugged his shoulders. "We'll have the chef get creative. And we will send out a hunting party for fresh venison. Father loves wild game, and that should distract him until the next shipment arrives."

Luka sighed, a frown transforming his features into concern.

"What's wrong?"

"Your Highness, we can't afford to send out a hunting party. Your father has every resource tracking down the rebels."

While peace between the borders of each sector existed, it was stretched thin and easily swayed to other sectors for the right price. The Southern Sector wasn't the poorest sector, but it was far from the most affluent and influential. Skirmishes still randomly popped up in the least-guarded areas. Luka was right. They couldn't pull guards from the borders—it would be a welcome invitation for more rebels to infiltrate.

"We can't sit here and not do anything." Liam took his suit jacket off and draped it across his desk chair. If they couldn't send a team of men, he'd do it himself. It had been ages since he'd walked through the woods near the castle. And he'd always enjoyed hunting with his father. With the stresses of his new engagement, the rebels, and the council pressuring him, the fresh air and wide-open skies would do him good.

"Meet me back here in a few minutes, and dress for the woods."

A smile spread across Luka's face. "We're going hunting?"

"That we are, Luka."

<h1 style="text-align:center;">Chapter Eleven</h1>

It took all of five minutes since Price Liam escorted Mia back to her rooms for the walls to start closing in. She'd never enjoyed sitting still, and there was nothing in the suite to occupy her time. Even if she had her cell phone, she doubted it would work. And so far, she had yet to see any computers or TVs —nothing resembling anything from her world.

If only she had her sketch pad. While she wasn't a master at drawing—her fingers itched to put pencil to paper. To do anything artistic. She thrived on creativity and color, and here, she hadn't found either.

Mia rummaged through the wardrobe for something more comfortable. The outing with Liam was a great diversion, but she was ready to get out of the multiple layers of fabric. She pulled a gray dress from the closet and tossed it onto the bed. Surely, she wouldn't have to bother calling Luna. After all, she'd been dressing herself since she was three.

Reaching her fingers around the lower part of her back, she tugged on the ribbon sash cinched at her waist. It came off easily enough, but now she had to reach for the zipper.

Wait—did they not use zippers here?

She raised her hands to the back of her neck, and sure enough —buttons.

Really? Who would want to sew buttons down the middle of a dress? They must have sewing machines for zippers. Mia unfastened the first three quickly, but the lower she worked, the harder it was to angle her arms and make her fingers cooperate with the small, slippery buttons. She glanced at the intercom and grunted in frustration. She did not want to bother Luna, especially over a silly thing like changing dresses.

Maneuvering to the mirror hanging beside her wardrobe, she finagled her body to get a look at the back of the dress. There weren't many more to go, and then she could wiggle it off her shoulders.

Determined, she set back to work, nearly popping her shoulder out of place in the process. But she kept on until the dress finally loosened enough to lower it. She had it halfway to the floor before it wouldn't go any farther.

"You've got to be kidding me." Mia blew a strand of hair, tickling her nose, and twisted the gown around—the insufferable buttons now in front of her.

"*Ha!*" She unbuttoned them, shimmied the dress to her feet, and then kicked it up to toss it on the bed as she stepped out of it. Her feet didn't quite make it out of the yards of fabric, and she landed in a heap on the floor, the layers a tangled mess around her ankles.

"Your Highness!"

Mia lifted her head from the wooden floor, cheeks burning at the sight of Luna in the doorway. She didn't even hear her come in.

"Why didn't you ring for me?"

She pushed herself up to a sitting position. "I didn't see a need."

Luna raised her eyebrow but said nothing as she closed the door and helped Mia to her feet. "Did you hurt anything?"

"You mean other than my pride?"

"Don't worry about that, Princess." The maid helped her step out of the dress and draped it over a chair. "I didn't see anything."

"I didn't want to bother you for a simple dress change."

Luna's hand froze inches from the gray dress on her bed. Her expression clouded for a few seconds. "That's my job."

The last thing Mia wanted was to insult possibly the only friend she'd made in the castle. "I suppose I'm not good at letting people help me." It wasn't a complete lie. Mia didn't enjoy asking anyone to help her—her independence was like a badge of honor she wore proudly.

"As the future queen, you will oversee the entire staff. You will have to learn how to rely on your servants."

She planned to be long gone before the wedding. But perhaps Luna was correct in a way. Mia needed other people in her life. Ones she could count on. An image of June filled her mind, and her throat tightened. June was her only family—her best friend. But even if she could get back home, she would have to find some way to widen her circle. June was married. She had a new husband, and they would start their own family one day.

"Are you all right, Your Highness?" Luna picked up the dress and walked over to her. "I apologize if I overstepped."

She blinked away her tears. "I'm fine. And you're right, of course. I will try to remember what you've said and make sure I call on you for help."

Appeased, Luna helped her step into the day dress and reached for more hairpins.

"Could you maybe braid it instead?" She rubbed the back of her neck, tension starting to tighten again.

"Another headache?"

"I can't seem to get these knots out of my shoulders." What she wouldn't give to be able to have a massage.

One by one, Luna pulled the bobby pins from the updo and let Mia's hair fall down her back. "Stress will do that to you." Luna sighed. "And you've certainly had your share of stress. I can't imagine what you've been through getting here."

Oh, no. Mia had tried so hard to avoid this topic since her arrival. And here, she practically opened the door and pushed Luna through it.

"Do you ever get severe headaches?" Mia peeked up at Luna to see her frown.

"Sometimes."

"What helps you get rid of them?" Mia prayed that Luna's answer would help her know if they had medicine or what they could do for her. Luna was right when she said it was stress-related. And no doubt that would only heighten the longer she was here and had to pretend she was someone she wasn't.

"Usually, I take medicine, maybe a hot shower or bath." Luna rummaged around in the vanity door. "If that doesn't work, I use oils and try to sleep."

Mia breathed a sigh of relief. All things she would do as well, and now she wouldn't look silly asking for medicine.

"Is there any way you can get some medicine?"

"Of course." Luna pulled a dark blue ribbon from the drawer. "I know you would like a braid, but royals usually wear their hair up. Especially at mealtimes."

"Well, can't I start my own traditions?" A smirk played at the corners of Luna's lips, so she quickly added. "It's just that my hair is so thick, it aggravates my headache when it's up."

"I think I can figure out some unique ways to braid it so it still looks elegant but hangs down."

"Thank you, Luna."

"You're welcome."

"Can you take me around the castle? I would love to explore a little."

"Bored already?" Luna teased, her eyes brightening. "What do you like to do?"

Surely, something crafty would be a safe bet since Luna made a living with jewelry. "I like to draw and paint."

Her face lit up. "You know what? I know of just the place."

Once her braid was finished, Mia slipped on her flats and

followed Luna into the hallway. Each time she left, it was impossible not to gawk at her surroundings and focus on which direction Luna was taking her.

Mia could not deny that the palace was beautiful, each room thoughtfully decorated in a humble but elegant way.

Once out of the royal wing, they crossed a sitting room, the ballroom, and headed toward the back of the castle. Servants bowed in her direction as she passed, but no one seemed curious enough to see where she was heading. Luna led her into a stairwell, and they climbed several flights of stairs before stopping in a small landing, just large enough for two people and a stone archway.

Luna held her hand out and pointed down the hallway. "Open the door on the left."

Mia nodded and dried her sweaty palms on the skirt of her dress. She did not know why she was suddenly so nervous. Her eyes caught another door on the right. "What's in there?"

"No one is allowed in that room." Her tone was firm and held no room for further questioning.

Mia turned the doorknob, her hand instantly grimy with dust, and pushed it open. Hinges squeaked and protested against the movement until it finally gave way. She almost stumbled across the rock floor.

Tears threatened to fill her eyes as she took in her surroundings. Floor-to-ceiling windows graced all three of the walls in front of her. It took a moment to pull her gaze away from the light streaming in through the layers of dust to notice the easels, tables, and tubes of paint that filled the floor in front of her. She whirled around to Luna, clapping her hands, unable to contain her excitement.

"It's an art studio!"

Her maid returned the grin. "Well, it certainly used to be."

"It would only take a little soap and elbow grease to fix it back up."

Luna's smile vanished. "It would take days to get this presentable again."

Reaching over, she gently tugged Luna closer to the window. "Just look at that view!"

Her servant's nose wrinkled up in disgust. "Make that a week."

"The gardens are down there, Luna. And just think about all the wonderful sunlight streaming in through these windows. I can't wait to create something."

"I will check with the main housekeeper and see if she can afford to let some girls come up here and get it presentable."

"Thank you!" Mia nearly squealed in delight but reigned in her excitement enough to keep her feet firmly on the ground. Somehow, she got the impression Luna wouldn't approve of a princess jumping up and down. Nor would she approve of her offer to help. Instead, she clamped her lips tight together and folded her hands in front of her.

A shrill beep chimed somewhere from Luna's apron, and the maid pulled out a small, rectangle device. The screen lit up, but Mia couldn't make out the words that scrolled by. "They need us at the queen's suite."

Mia hadn't officially met Prince Liam's parents, and the idea of him not being present sent her mind whirling in a thousand directions.

"Don't worry. This room's not going anywhere."

She nodded and followed Luna out of the studio and back down the stone stairs. It wasn't the studio she was worried about.

Chapter Twelve

"I don't understand why we must do all this extra work. What kind of princess shows up for her engagement and doesn't bring her own clothes and personal items?"

Luna bit the inside of her cheek to prevent saying a snarky reply to one of the queen's maids, Elsie. It wouldn't do to create drama between her and the other lady's maids. Especially since Elsie technically outranked her.

When she escorted Amelia to the queen's suite a few hours ago, a seamstress was waiting, tools in hand, to measure and create an entire wardrobe for Princess Amelia. Luna noticed the look of relief on Amelia's face when the queen excused herself a few minutes later, putting the princess in the capable hands of the designer and several maids. While the designer would handle the more complicated gowns, the maids were asked to make day dresses and nightgowns.

Luna hoped Princess Amelia was faring better than she was at the moment.

She took her foot off the sewing machine pedal and quietly replied, "Something must have happened to her belongings."

"Do you know?" Elsie brightened, no doubt expecting gossip. "Has she told you?"

"No, she hasn't, and it isn't my place to ask."

"Well, there's no reason to get so high and mighty—*Luna*." The maid drew out her name in a sneer. "Some of us are confidants of those we serve. I just assumed you would be since you were brought to the palace."

Ouch. Luna figured there might be some jealousy issues with her arriving to tend to Princess Amelia. She didn't expect the open hostility. Not for the first time since arriving at the palace, she longed to return to her studio apartment over her shop.

Instead of satisfying the maid with another reply, she ignored her completely, focusing on the collar of the day dress she was making for the princess.

"That's enough, Elsie." Queen Scarlett's head maid ordered, barely raising her gaze from her machine.

Elsie narrowed her eyes in Luna's direction but didn't say another word.

Even though Elsie rubbed her the wrong way, she wasn't entirely wrong. Most lady's maids eventually have the ear of their mistresses. But that would come over time—something Luna didn't have. Getting to know Amelia and letting her open up on her own wouldn't work since Luna had Mr. Ortega breathing down her neck to keep this massive secret.

How could she convince the girl to trust and confide in her? And even more—keep everyone else from discovering the truth? If she'd noticed the many times this "princess" had either said or done something out of character, how long would it be before someone who mattered saw it?

And *she* was not an expert on the actions of royalty.

Luna blew a strand of hair from her eyes and bent over the machine. There was not room for doubts right now. She would simply have to use whatever knowledge she could pry from her memory about the Western Sector and teach it to Amelia. Of course, there was also the library. She could dig up some information from there as well.

She finished the last few stitches on the collar and cut it from the machine. There. Another dress finished. She hung it on the rolling rack with the other garments. All things considered, they were progressing well with the dress-making. This set of clothes would give the princess a decent start on a wardrobe until the designer's workers finished the other designs.

Before long, the future queen would have a beautiful collection.

"Are you done already?" Elsie looked up from her machine, a frown forming on her lips.

"Yes, for today." Luna rotated her neck, trying to work out the stiffness. "I have to go get Princess Amelia ready for dinner."

"You should have said something!" The Queen's maid, Piper, jumped up from the desk, her dress still attached to the machine, but she just left it on the table. "I can't be late. Come on, Elsie."

"I'll follow you both out."

The maid raised her hand in a wave as she dashed down the servant's hall, tying her apron back on her dress in the process. Luna's hands automatically went to her waist to smooth out wrinkles, but nothing was attached to her dress.

Looking down, she groaned. She must have left her apron in the workroom. She turned on her heel and picked up her pace. Now, she would be the late one.

"Can you believe Luna is the new Princess's maid?"

She stopped in the doorway and peered into the room. Two maids were left working, no doubt cleaning maids who were pulled in to help with the dresses.

"Exactly. You would think they would have offered the job to someone who works at the castle." A maid with pretty red curls responded, bitterness dripping from her words.

"I know. Poor Elsie was so upset." The other maid agreed. "She's the one who should have been Princess Amelia's maid."

Not wanting to hear another word, Luna cleared her throat and walked into the room. Both of the maids jumped at the sight of her.

"I forgot my apron."

"Can't forget that." The first maid said, and Luna couldn't tell if she was trying to appear friendly or sarcastic. Either way, she knew now never to try a friendship with these two. Or Elsie.

She scooped up the apron from her station and smiled over her shoulder at them. "Must be such an honor to be pulled up here to sew for the princess, *huh*?"

It was petty. But as she walked past the duo—their mouths hanging open in shock—she lifted her head high and grinned.

Chapter Thirteen

"We are late, Your Highness."

Liam glanced at the clock in his sitting room and sighed. "It will be fine, Luka."

"Are you sure about that?" Luka reached out with a towel in his hands and stopped the prince from walking out the door. "Your hair is dripping water on your collar."

"I couldn't show up to dinner smelling like a deer carcass."

"No, I don't suppose you should." His servant frowned but continued to dab off the back of his neck. "But what excuse will you give your mother when she asks why you are dripping all over the tablecloths?"

"She may think it's funny."

"I hardly think the queen will approve of your disheveled appearance." He gestured to Liam's shirt tale. "You haven't even tucked in your shirt!"

"Oh, no, the world's coming to an end." Liam took one look at Luka's scowl and tucked in the garment. Teasing Luka was fun, but he respected the man enough not to go too far toward disrespect. "Better?"

"Just for your information, the world *did* end—or don't you remember a little thing called the Tenebrous Era?" He held up a dark gray dinner jacket for Liam to slip on. "And yes, that is much better."

Liam slid his arm into the sleeve. "Luka, I've never known you to tell a joke in my entire life."

"Perhaps His Highness's humor is rubbing off on me."

Liam adjusted the jacket sleeves, held out both arms to the side, and grinned. "There. Am I presentable now?"

Luka's bushy eyebrows furrowed together. "You'll do."

"Well, let's not keep everyone waiting. I can only imagine what questions my father will interrogate the princess with in my delay."

That thought spurred his feet into action. Liam sprinted out of his room and down the hallway, nearly running into a servant carrying a stack of folded laundry. He called, "I'm sorry!" over his shoulder but continued his speed down the staircase and across the main floor toward the dining room.

He skidded to a stop in front of the door, ran a hand through his hair, adjusted his jacket, and pushed open the door.

"Well, finally," Father grumbled, getting to his feet. "Shall we?"

Liam let his gaze move from his father and his mother's disapproving frown to land on Princess Amelia. Her eyes lifted to meet his, her features easing into a relieved smile. He silently scolded himself for being so late. He knew how uncomfortable he would feel if the situation had been reversed. Determining not to let that happen again, he offered Amelia his arm.

"I'm sorry I am late."

"Well, you're here now, dear." Mother patted his arm on her way out the door. "But I'm afraid had you taken any longer, your father would have started without you."

"I'm not surprised." Liam followed his parents across the hall and led Amelia to the dining room table. A servant held the chair out for her on his left, and he stood while another seated his mother across from him. Once both ladies were seated, he took his place, and seconds later, the first course was set on the table.

No doubt the palace chef was stressed as well because of his tardiness.

"Is everything all right?" Concern filled Amelia's quiet voice as he turned to meet her gaze.

"Of course." He tried to put her at ease, but her brow furrowed.

"No, I mean—earlier." She lowered her voice to a whisper. "When you had to rush out of our picnic."

The rebels. "It's complicated." A glance in his father's direction determined he might not be staring, but he was, in fact, listening. "Princess Amelia, I was wondering if you would like to take a walk in the gardens after dinner?"

Pink tinted her cheeks, but she seemed to follow his changing the subject. "That would be lovely. Thank you."

His parents dominated the conversation, which was fine with Liam. He didn't know what to say to make this whole thing any less awkward. He tried to see things through Princess Amelia's eyes. New surroundings, new people, and a new culture.

Dinner with a family that would become her new family. He didn't know if he could do it. If he could leave the only life he knew, trade it for a brand new one, and be expected to join in on the small talk as if this happened all the time.

Liam took a moment to steal a glance at Amelia. One hand held her fork, picking at the remnants of the grilled chicken breast, while her other hand clenched her napkin in her lap. Perhaps they moved too fast, asking her to join them at family dinners.

"What do you think about taking that walk now?"

Her fork halted to a stop on her plate.

Mother's voice interrupted their conversation. "Liam, dessert hasn't been served yet."

"I think I'd like that, Your Highness," Amelia replied before he could contradict his mother's opinion.

"Perfect." He signaled the servant over. "Would you please

bring the dessert to the gardens in a few minutes? We will have it on the patio."

The servant bowed. "Of course, Your Highness."

"Thank you." He stood, placing his napkin on his plate, and held out a hand for Amelia. It wasn't until they were outside that he felt Amelia physically relax.

"Better?"

"Yes, thank you."

"I'm sorry I didn't think about how hard this would be on you."

"I suppose this isn't a normal occurrence. It's hard to know exactly what to do—or not to do, for that matter."

"Regardless—going forward, I will try to be more thoughtful of your feelings. Perhaps we could have dinner together, and once you're more comfortable, we can try formal family meals again."

"I'd like that." Tears glistened in her bright blue eyes. "Thank you for being so kind."

"If anyone understands how intimidating the king and queen are, it's me." He pointed to the patio table in the center of the garden. "Looks like they already have the table ready."

A vase filled with fresh-cut flowers, no doubt ones from this garden, stood in the center of the wrought-iron table. An antique oil lamp lit up the patio, casting light over the rose bushes.

"It's beautiful."

"Come on, let's see what they left us."

Two pieces of cheesecake—one chocolate and one strawberry —sat in front of their seats. "Which one would you like?" Liam gestured to the plates, letting her pick first.

"*Hmm.*" Amelia looked at the strawberry in front of her and then grinned at his piece of chocolate. "How about we cut them in half and share?"

"Princess Amelia, I like the way you think." He cut his half and slid it onto her plate, and she did the same. Her grin was contagious, and Liam smiled back at her.

"Tell me something about you." He took a bite of the cheesecake and waited.

"Like what?"

"Anything at all." He racked his brain for a suggestion. "What's your greatest fear?"

Amelia coughed and picked up her water goblet. "Why don't we start with something a little easier?"

She was right. That was a tough one. He laughed and soaked his cheesecake in the strawberry syrup on his plate. "I'm sorry. I'm not very good at this."

"Me either, so don't worry." She set down her cup and sighed. "Let's see. How about something we enjoy doing?"

"Okay, fine. That seems a little easier." He teased. "You go first."

"I like eating cheesecake." She gave him a grin that lit up her entire face, and Liam laughed.

"*Hmm*, didn't see that one coming."

"Fine. I love dessert." She scooped up a forkful of the chocolate slice and waved it at him. "Chocolate is my favorite. But cheesecake, cookies, chocolate-covered strawberries—now those are divine—and I've been known to eat my dessert first on many occasions."

"Mother wouldn't know what to do if you did that." He tried to imagine her face if the servants brought out the dessert first. It was such a funny image, he decided he'd have to try it sometime.

"Life is too short to not enjoy it."

"Touché." He leaned back in the chair and looked up at the sky. The moon was nearly full, lighting up the trees more than usual. A cool, gentle breeze shuffled the leaves in the trees, the rustling sound bringing a sense of peace he hadn't experienced in a while.

Did his parents ever experience this? This quiet, comfortable conversation when they were getting to know each other. He wouldn't believe it if anyone had told him a week ago that he would enjoy himself so much with a woman he barely knew.

Did his parents ever appreciate the little things in life? Did he? Princess Amelia had one thing correct—life was too short. His days were full of negotiating, worry, and decisions. Maybe he could get used to sitting out here, eating dessert, and talking about anything and everything that didn't have anything to do with running the palace.

What would it be like to look forward to the little things in life? Like splitting two different types of dessert with his fiancée?

The wind played with the wisps of hair around her face, and he wondered what it would be like to brush a strand away from her cheek.

"Did I say something to upset you?" Amelia's soft voice brought him back to reality.

He froze, realizing he had been quiet for too long and that she caught him staring.

"No." He gave her a reassuring smile and looked back down at his plate, finishing the last of his cheesecake. "I'm just enjoying the evening."

Chapter Fourteen

True to his word, Prince Liam ate dinner with Mia alone for the rest of the week. They would sit in the small breakfast room or outside under the stars. He never mentioned what his parents thought of the arrangement, and she didn't want to bring it up. But the thoughtful gesture went a long way to soothe her anxiety over this whole situation.

Sometimes, their conversations flowed nicely, and other times, Mia didn't know what to say and clammed up. Too afraid of being caught saying something she shouldn't.

The prince must have a lot of patience because he never once showed that the lack of conversation bothered him. Either that, or he was bored with her presence already and looked forward to the silence.

It seemed hard to believe she had already been at the palace for almost a week. She spent her days in the abandoned art studio. With the help of a few maids, it was almost like brand new. Dust and grime were gone, and with the sunlight streaming in through the massive windows, time spent there became the bright spot of her day. The servants insisted on bringing flowers to fill the empty spaces. The bare floor boasted a new rug, and in the far-left corner sat a small table and chairs—on Luna's order. She claimed without it, Mia wouldn't stop to go downstairs for lunch.

Which was probably true.

When Mia took on a new project, it consumed her entire focus until it was finished. Then she would sit and sulk for a while, moving here and there between projects until her fingers itched to pick up the brush again, and a new obsession began. June always shook her head at Mia's creative process but never made fun of her for it. If anything, June encouraged Mia to refine her craft and expand out of her comfort zone.

If there were a new craft class in the area, June would put both of their names on the list.

"Princess Amelia, are you in here?"

Mia startled at Luna's voice coming from the doorway. She dried her eyes and turned around, plastering a smile on her face. "Yes, Luna."

"Good. I've been looking for you." Her maid crossed over to the window and stood beside her, raising her eyebrow. Mia looked down at the stool and easel she drug across the floor and propped next to the center of the window.

"What? I wanted to have a closer look at the gardens."

"There's nothing on your canvas."

"I know. I was just about to get started."

Her maid danced right there in front of her. "Well, that will have to wait because you have to come with me and get ready."

"For what?"

"For your date with Prince Liam to the theater."

Now, whose turn was it to raise her eyebrow? She sighed at Luna's excitement, but a tiny thrill filled her stomach. "It's not a date."

"Fine. Your *outing* with Prince Liam. Is that better?"

"Much."

"Come on. Let's go get you ready." Luna led the way back to Mia's bedroom.

A light blue velvet dress lay across her bed. Mia gently ran a hand over the soft fabric and then waited for Luna to help her dress and fix her hair.

"You're quiet tonight," Luna said, brushing through Mia's blonde waves.

"Sorry. I'm just thinking about the Way of Light Festival coming up."

Luna brightened. "*Ah*, yes. It's such an important step in your engagement."

It might be important, but Luna didn't know anything about it. She thought she would have been home by now, but she couldn't return to the chapel. She was never alone and did not know if she could manage to slip out of the castle undetected. Now, another event was almost here, and she had no idea what to expect. Her stomach roiled at the thought of getting dressed up, facing an enormous crowd, and Liam's parents unprepared.

Before she could chicken out, Mia leaned forward and stood from the chair. She whirled around to Luna and blurted, "What is the Way of Light Festival?"

Luna's face paled. Her eyes widened as she backed away from the table and hurried to the sitting-room door of her suite.

"Please, Luna. I need your help."

Luna bolted the lock on the door and turned around. "I know." She motioned for Mia to follow her back into the bedroom and sit on the bed. "I don't know who you are, and frankly, I don't want to know."

The room spun.

Mia lowered herself down on the bed beside Luna. "How long have you known that I'm not—"

"Don't say it!" Luna clamped her hand over Mia's mouth. "Never admit that out loud."

She nodded, and Luna removed her hand. "Shortly after you arrived."

Tears filled her eyes. "I didn't know what to do. They mistook me for her, and I had nowhere else to go. I'm all alone—and I was scared."

Luna's eyes softened a tiny bit. "I believe you wouldn't have done it unless you had no other option."

"Thank you."

"I can't tell you all the details of how I know, and I don't want you to tell me yours. That would only put both of us in more danger. It's safer for both of us to know the bare minimum. Understand?"

No words came, so Mia just nodded.

"Now that is out of the way, the most important thing to do is make sure that no one else finds out about this."

"You're not going to tell Prince Liam?"

Luna shook her head. "No, I'm not. No good would come from that now."

A nagging sensation settled into the bottom of her stomach, and Mia got the feeling that there was definitely more to the story than Luna shared. The memory of Luna's red and bruised forearms sprang to her mind. "Luna, is that why you were bruised the other day? Is someone hurting you because of this?"

"No details, remember?"

Mia couldn't bear it if someone else was physically harmed because of her lie. "I'm sorry. This is just all so much."

"I know. For me too." Luna reached over and clasped her hand. "But we are going to get through this together."

"Thank you."

"Don't thank me yet. From what I've witnessed, you know absolutely nothing about being a royal."

Ouch. Even though it was true, the admission stung just a little. Mia thought she'd done a good job so far—okay—a halfway decent job at pretending to be a royal. But what could she say without giving too many details? Even without that rule firmly established, Luna would never believe she came from a different time. Perhaps this would be a blessing, though. She could learn all she could without worrying about tripping up and revealing too much.

"You're correct—I don't."

Luna leaned back but didn't let go of her hand. Clearly, she expected that answer, but perhaps the truth stung her just as much. "Well, we will have to find a safe place to talk, and I'm not sure the palace is a good idea. There are always ears listening. The last thing we need is for someone to eavesdrop." Luna got to her feet and paced the room.

"We can't talk freely in here?"

"Possibly. But I don't know if it's worth the risk."

Mia didn't like the idea of her own sitting room not being private. Was there some sort of a listening device she didn't know of? And who would want to listen to her conversations anyway?

"Okay, how about the gardens?"

"Better. But there are too many servants going in and out. Plus, the queen loves her roses. She's always out there."

"What about your shop?"

The girl brightened. "That might work. But coming up with a reason to go there … I'm not sure it would be that easy."

"It's no secret that I admire your jewelry. Maybe you could show me how to make a bracelet. Which would be something I would normally want to do anyway." She folded her hands in her lap and looked away. "Plus, the fewer lies that pile up, the better."

"I don't like lies either." Luna's voice was soft and understanding. "I think that would work, but we would have some guard sent with us, I'm sure."

"Surely, this guard wouldn't be in the room the whole time."

"You're probably right." Luna sighed. "I think it's our best bet. But for now, we need to get you downstairs."

Getting to her feet, she let Luna fuss over her dress and hair one last time. Once the servant deemed her ready to go, Luna opened the door and curtsied. "Off you go, my Lady. Your Prince awaits."

Chapter Fifteen

How was he supposed to get to know his fiancée when she sat quietly beside him and didn't initiate any conversation? They arrived at the theater early. Plenty of time to get to their seats in the royal box, relax, and talk before the actors took the stage.

It wasn't as if he wasn't trying to communicate with Princess Amelia. He asked her a few polite questions, and she answered but gave nothing further. She was quiet at their dinners together as well, but he'd hoped it might make things easier since they were away from the palace.

How did his ancestors ever get through these arranged marriages? Since the Tenebrous Era, marriage for love was rare. Most couples married for the simplicity of aligning their resources —food, shelter, and what little money circulated throughout the Southern Sector. But even before the Tenebrous Era, way back in the 1920s, his ancestors who had settled in what was once the United States also had a marriage of convenience. It worked out for them. There had been generation after generation of Dunnes. The family tree was now so big that Liam had to put large pieces of paper together to track them all.

But even though marrying for love was rare—he'd still hoped

he would find it. Could he find love with the woman sitting beside him?

He stole a glance at Princess Amelia, who was absentmindedly brushing her long hair off her shoulder. While royals and courtiers tended to always have their hair up in some fancy design, she stuck to braids and usually with most of her hair hanging down. Only the working class wore such hairstyles. But Amelia's braids weren't just braids. They were entwined with ribbons and carefully crafted in elegant designs.

He cleared his throat and looked away, mentally shaking himself. Here he was debating hairstyles. What was wrong with him? But even he couldn't deny that he preferred this new way she wore hers.

Liam blamed it on the wayward thoughts of love. He was too wrapped up in what he'd hoped to have one day. He was engaged to a stranger, so he'd better get used to it.

The lights dimmed and then flickered. A signal that the play was about to start. He took another glance at the brochure and sighed—a comedy. At least there wouldn't be a romance story to further carry his ridiculous thoughts toward love.

As the curtain lifted, Amelia looked over at him and grinned. He grinned right back at her—the excitement in her eyes was contagious.

So much for forgetting about romance.

Two hours later, Liam was on his feet, clapping with the rest of the audience. The actors were wonderful, but he found himself more engrossed with Amelia's reactions to the play. He was amused by how she enjoyed the show—how when she found something hilarious, she laughed so hard that tears ran down her cheeks.

The door to the royal box opened. Luka and Luna entered but waited in the back of the room. The crowd's noise died down, and Liam found himself not ready for the night to end.

He wanted to hear the princess laugh some more. To let down her guarded walls and talk to him. To have a friendship with the woman he was supposed to spend the rest of his life with.

"What would you say to a late dinner at Mrs. Vera's tonight instead of rushing back to the palace?"

It took her a moment to answer, but she finally rewarded him with a smile. "I'd like that."

"Great." He motioned for Luka to come over. "Would you please let Mrs. Vera know we will stop by?"

"Of course, Your Highness." He motioned for a guard, and they were on the way down the stairs and to the back of the theater. "You know, we will need to give Mrs. Vera a little notice to prepare a table for us. Would you like to walk down to the marketplace for a few minutes?"

She instantly brightened. "That sounds lovely."

Instead of getting into the royal car, Liam offered his arm, and they walked down a quiet street to the nearest crosswalk. One more block over, and they would be at the market.

Most vendors were already closed for the evening, but a few shops stayed open, perhaps hoping viewers from the theater would make their way over.

Even though the princess seemed excited about the marketplace, she remained silent. Liam couldn't stand it any longer. He stopped and faced her. "Princess Amelia, is there something wrong?"

Denial filled her eyes. "No. Of course not."

"Are you sure? Because you haven't said two sentences all evening." Clearing his throat, he tried a different approach. He wanted friendship, not to scare her away from him. "Have I done or said something to make you uncomfortable?"

"No, not at all." Her hand found his, and she gave it a squeeze. "You're a perfect gentleman, as always."

Liam glanced down at her hand on top of hers and wondered what it would be like to entwine his fingers with hers. To feel her soft palm against his. Lifting his gaze, he also found her staring down at their hands. A soft red blush spread across her cheek.

You want friendship, Liam. Nothing more. Before he thought about it, he gently lifted her hand and guided it back to the crook of his elbow.

"Well, I don't know about you, but all that laughing this evening has made me famished."

"It was nice to take a break and just have fun."

"Indeed. I'm afraid lately I haven't taken much time to do anything other than work."

"My sister always says that's the fastest way to achieve burnout."

"Burnout?"

She cleared her throat before continuing. "When you tire of doing what you do every day and have no more passion or energy for it, you can become cynical about it."

Burnout was a word he hadn't heard used in a long time. It was an older term—much older—from before the Tenebrous Era.

"There you two are!" Mrs. Vera rushed out the door and scooped them both up in a hug. "My favorite royal couple."

She leaned back, studying each of their faces. "Something's the matter, but don't worry. There's nothing that a little dinner and dessert can't fix."

She hurried back into the restaurant, gesturing for them to follow her toward the kitchen. But just before they reached it, she pulled back a curtain to reveal a small room that had no doubt been set up in a hurry. A few boxes still sat in the corner, but the rest of the room was empty except for a table for two. Complete with a vase of flowers and two tapered candles.

"From now on, this room will be specifically for the beautiful couple." Mrs. Vera beamed. "It's even by the back door, in case you need to escape." She winked and laughed. Delight lighting up her eyes.

"You did not have to go to so much trouble, Mrs. Vera." Liam pulled out a seat for Amelia. "But it's perfect."

"Yes. Thank you so much." Amelia touched the daisies, gracing the center of the table. "It is perfect."

"Well, next time, it will be even nicer. I will have it painted and decorated." She wiped her hands on her apron and then pulled out a notepad. "Tonight, my special is a cheesy potato soup and fresh baked bread."

"What's for dessert?" Liam asked, peaking at Amelia from the corner of his eye. He wanted to see her reaction.

"Powered donuts with a chocolate dipping sauce."

"That sounds amazing." Amelia grinned. "All of it."

"It certainly does." How did Mrs. Vera get her hands on chocolate? He knew that the latest few shipments of goods were all essentials—not frivolous and luxurious like chocolate. It was hard enough for the royal chef to acquire something so rare, let alone a working-class chef.

"Mrs. Vera, I think we will have our dessert first."

Amelia gasped. "Prince Liam, I think I'm rubbing off on you."

He turned his attention from Mrs. Vera back to his companion. Gone was the tension and stress of her posture and face, and in its place, she seemed relaxed—happy, even. Princess Amelia was becoming increasingly hard to figure out, and now he had one more mystery added to the list.

Where was Mrs. Vera getting her food supplies? Apprehension gnawed in his gut. He couldn't even bring himself to think of Mrs. Vera and rebels together in the same sentence. Would he have to investigate his favorite person from childhood?

Chapter Sixteen

"I don't know what came over me last night, Luna, but the prince must think I'm an idiot."

"What makes you say that?" Luna grabbed her key from the silver chain around her neck and unlocked her shop's door.

"I was awkward, quiet, and weird." Princess Amelia—or whatever her real name was—chewed on her lower lip before adding, "But when we ate together at Mrs. Vera's, I was relaxed and talkative. Flirty, even."

Luna pushed open the door to the shop and gave it a good surveillance glance before ushering the young lady in. The guard who escorted them—a tall young man with dark brown eyes and a dimple on his chin—followed, closing the door behind them.

"I'm going to check upstairs. Stay here before you go up." The guard walked past them and toward the back, where the stairs to her private apartment were located.

"I don't know. I feel like he knows something I do not, and it's all some game that I'm failing."

She grabbed the girl's arm and shushed her. "Wait until we lose the guard."

"Of course. I'm sorry."

"Why don't I show you my supply room? That will give something to talk about until he comes back down."

"Sounds great."

Luna led the way behind her counter, past the stairs and into a room she transformed from a linen closet to a storage closet. Rows of beads, jewels, and wires were stacked neatly on the shelves above a long piece of wood she'd nailed to the wall as a desk.

"Luna, this is so amazing!" Amelia reached out and pulled a box of beads down. "These are beautiful."

"Thank you." Embarrassed, Luna pulled out two stools pushed under the makeshift desk. "Have a seat, and I'll show you how to make a simple bracelet."

Amelia's eyes lit up. "Like a friendship bracelet?"

"A what?"

"Oh, you must not have them here." Amelia whispered, "It's something kids give to their friends. Usually made from some type of thread or leather. To symbolize their friendship."

"We have something similar here." Luna went back to the shelf and searched for the correct bin. "Here." She set it on the table in front of Amelia. "These are Family Ties."

Footsteps in the hall alerted they weren't alone, so she held up a finger.

"Everything is all clear, Princess Amelia." His gaze roamed over the two of them and back to the princess. "I will wait for you both outside and make sure you're not disturbed."

"Thank you, Jake."

The guard bowed. "Princess Amelia." And then his eyes moved to Luna's and held them while he nodded to her. "Luna."

A giggle burst from Amelia after the guard left, drawing Luna's attention back to the table. "I think someone may have an admirer."

"Don't be silly."

"Oh, come on. It's obvious. But if you don't want to talk

about it, I understand." She picked up a dark blue stone. "Now, what is Family Tie jewelry?"

"It's a gift that your whole family wears to show that you're a part of something larger than yourself." Luna pushed up her sleeve and held up her wrist. "Some make necklaces, some rings, some bracelets. My father and I have bracelets."

"When the Tenebrous Era happened, it became increasingly hard to keep up with family—especially extended family. Communication lines went down. No one could call or email. Devices and phones became a thing of the past. And only the royals or extremely wealthy persons had working tablets or phones."

Luna touched the green and yellow leather woven bracelet and turned it around her wrist, showing Amelia the silver charm hanging from it. "Eventually, as years passed and distant family members grew up, you had no proof that you were who you said you were. So, families started designing Family Ties. They picked two colors and a style, with an engraving of their last name, and gave one to everyone in the family that they could find as a way to identify them."

"Do people still do this?"

"It's not as practiced as it was in the beginning. So don't worry that you don't have one."

Amelia sighed. "Good. One less thing that I have to worry about."

"Okay, so let's go over the Way of Light Festival." Luna cleared the table of the Family Ties jewels and brought back a bin of simple ropes and colorful leather. She sat out a few pieces for each of them in case Jake interrupted them again.

"The Way of Light Festival is the second ceremony in your engagement. They hold it in the marketplace square at dusk. Everyone, from the poor all the way to the courtiers, will be there. And, of course, the royal family."

The princess flinched but didn't say anything as Luna picked up three strands of leather and cut them to equal lengths. "Can you braid?"

"Yes, of course." Amelia picked out three round jewels, and Luna raised an eyebrow at her choices. They were all brightly colored. Teal, purple, and bright green.

"Back to the Festival." Luna sighed, starting her bracelet out of a dull green. She'd braid a few strands, thread a bead, and then continue the braid. Surprisingly, Amelia was a quick study. But if the girl could paint, she would undoubtedly be talented in other areas.

"The festival is for the people, but it's also a way for the royal couple to work together and build their lantern. They write their wishes for their people and their sector and place the wishes inside of the lantern."

Amelia's eyes widened at the news, but looked eager to know more. "We build the lantern together?"

"Yes, and then you release it together in front of the people. The king will say a few words, then Prince Liam and you will tell the people what you wished."

"That sounds beautiful."

"It really is." Luna nodded to the bracelet. "And you are a fast student."

"Thanks. I love to make things. Pretty much anything creative is up my alley."

Luna grinned. Her earlier suspicions were correct. Princess Amelia had the gift of creating. "I can tell."

"Do you mind if I make one more?"

"Of course not, go ahead."

"Thanks." Amelia pulled matching leather out of the bin and set to work on another bracelet. This time, leaving out the black beads except for two. She placed them both in the center of the bracelet.

After a few minutes of silence, Princess Amelia asked, "Does the Princess of the Western Sector have a sister?"

Luna looked up in surprise. "Princess Amelia, do you know anything about the Western Sector?"

Amelia set down her bracelet. "No."

"I see." This was going to be harder than she originally thought. There was a lot more going on than Luna realized. She took a deep breath, trying to organize her thoughts. "Okay, so you are telling me you don't know anything about being a royal or anything about the Western Sector?"

The girl's voice was so soft that Luna almost couldn't hear her. "Luna, I'm not from your time."

Chapter Seventeen

Late morning sun streamed in through the sheer curtains in her royal bedroom. Mia pulled the blankets over her head, covering herself in darkness. Of all the stupid things for her to admit to, she'd opened her big mouth and blabbed the one thing Luna told her she didn't want to know. Specifics.

Of course, Luna sat and stared at her like Mia had sprouted a second head. And to make matters worse, she even told Luna she guessed that her time period was from just before the Tenebrous Era. To which Luna grew entirely pale and forcibly put a finger to her lips for her to stop talking.

Mia couldn't deny how the weight lifted off her shoulders at her revelation of the truth, though. She'd felt so much better—lighter even—than when she stepped foot into the dilapidated chapel that day.

To have at least one person know her secret made her feel like herself again. It was short-lived however, because immediately Luna told her not to say another word about it and promptly changed the subject back to the Way of Light Festival.

Lifting her arm, she admired the new bracelet encircling her wrist. Each color represented a part of herself. Teal for her favorite color, purple for June to symbolize her past, and green, the one color in the art studio that she couldn't stop from moving for first. Turning over, she reached under the pillow and pulled out the second bracelet. Similar but different—more masculine than feminine. She had only one person in mind when she made it. Prince Liam.

What prompted her to make him one, she had no idea. But now, she was embarrassed to even think about giving it to him. Perhaps she got caught up in Luna's Family Tie story and saw the meaning and similarity to her friendship bracelet. A Family Tie?

Nonsense. Her family was June and her new husband, Mark.

Prince Liam was not her family and never would be. She wouldn't be here long enough for that to happen. Of that, she was certain.

She shoved the bracelet back under her pillow, along with her shame and worry. How was she going to pull this off long enough to come up with a plan to escape? The longer this went on, the bigger the chance for friendship and feelings to blossom and people to get hurt. That was the last thing she wanted to do.

Prince Liam didn't deserve to get hurt.

But then again, she didn't either—right?

Was it wrong to look out for herself? To make sure she was taken care of? What if there wasn't a way back home, and she was stuck in this new and strange time? She couldn't stay in the palace, but maybe she could travel to another sector, set up an art studio, and support herself.

The door of her sitting room opened and closed, and footsteps clacked against the wooden floor. She sank deeper into the blankets. Maybe Luna would leave her alone and let her sleep.

The footsteps stopped, and whoever was there sighed before ripping the blanket from her.

"Hey!" She squinted against the bright light and fought to reach for the covers, but Luna tossed them aside.

"What are you doing? It's almost lunchtime."

"So?"

"You have to be down in the gardens in thirty minutes to meet Prince Liam."

The lantern. She totally forgot they had to build the lantern today. "I'm sorry, it slipped my mind."

"Come on, I brought you some toast and jam. I figured you hadn't eaten anything when you didn't touch your breakfast tray this morning."

"Thank you, Luna."

The maid gave her a small smile. "Get up and grab a slice of toast while I pick out your dress."

Mia pulled herself off the silky sheets and slid her feet into the slippers waiting at the end of the bed. Some things about the palace life she could get used to. She would definitely miss the comfortable bed and fuzzy shoes when she left.

"Why were you still in bed? Another headache?"

Mia lathered on what appeared to be homemade strawberry jam and took a bite. "This is amazing."

"Haven't you had jam and toast before?"

"It's not common to have it homemade."

Luna's face scrunched up in confusion but then waved the comment away. "You didn't answer my original question."

"Oh, right." She picked up a glass of water and took a sip. "No headache today. I just couldn't sleep. I felt terrible about what happened last night."

Luna pulled a dark purple dress from the wardrobe. "Don't worry about it." She helped Mia slip on the dress and pulled the ribboned sash around her back. "Just don't bring that up again." Her voice was barely audible. "Even though I'm really curious now."

Mia smiled. At least her one and only friend didn't seem to be angry with her. "I'm curious about so much as well." She took her spot in front of the vanity and watched as Luna added a single black ribbon to her hair, letting her tresses flow down without a braid or updo.

"I thought this wasn't allowed?" she asked, running a hand down the silky waves.

"You're the princess, so why don't you be yourself?" She bent down and whispered. "But just with your hair."

Mia laughed, appreciating the small gesture. "Alrighty, let's go build a lantern."

"Let's." Luna opened the door and led the way down the stairs and through the many hallways throughout the main floor to get to the gardens.

Prince Liam was already seated but got to his feet as soon as Mia stepped foot onto the patio.

"Princess Amelia, hello."

Should she curtsey? Considering Liam didn't bow toward her like he did at mealtimes, she gave him a wide smile. "Good afternoon, Prince Liam."

"Are you ready to make this lantern?" He eyed the table littered with supplies with a suspicious look. "Because I do not know what I'm doing."

"It's a good thing you have me, then."

"I guess it is." His look nearly froze Mia to her spot. Sincerity and warmth poured from his eyes, and her traitor heart fluttered in her chest. She couldn't get close to him. She couldn't. It would be too painful when she had to leave.

"Well, let's take a look at what we've got." She finally found her footing and met him at the table. Paint sat to the side, along with brushes and stencils. A blank paper lantern graced the middle of the table.

"We could paint it and maybe draw on a design?"

"We could put our initials on the side," Liam added, picking up a tube of green paint. Her heart fluttered again at his choice.

"Sounds perfect," she said, grabbing the purple. Before she could even pour the paint on her plate, a servant appeared, pulling an apron over her head. "*Oh!*"

"Sorry, Princess Amelia." The young girl blushed. "I didn't want you to get paint on your dress."

"Good thinking." She smiled at the girl and waited while she tied the string into a knot in the back. "Don't laugh, Your Highness. You'll need one too."

"I do, *huh*? I'm not one to spill things on myself." He raised an eyebrow but let the young servant pull one over his head.

"It doesn't matter whether you intend to or not. Paint has a way of going where it wants to."

"I will take your word for it." Liam picked up a brush with a glob of green paint and dotted her cheek. "You got some paint right there." He pointed to his cheek.

"Oh, I do, do I?" Mia dipped her finger in the purple and lunged for his nose. "There, that's much better."

"You better run," Liam warned, picking up an entire bottle of paint.

"You wouldn't dare!"

"I wouldn't?" He teased, his eyes wrinkling up in the corners. "One."

Mia halted, unsure of what to do.

"Two."

Squealing, she grabbed her own bottle just as he shouted, "Three!" They squirted paint on each other at the same time and paused, no doubt shocked that the other had actually gone through with it.

Before Mia could say anything, Liam grabbed another bottle and sprayed her with both at the same time. She gasped, running around the table as he chased her. She grabbed a large brush, swiped paint from a plate, and then flung the paint, coating his arm.

A full-out paint fight ensued until both laughed so hard that Mia had tears running down her cheeks.

"Okay, truce?" Liam managed to call out, reaching out to stop her hand as she dipped her brush down in the paint once more.

Mia rose from the table as Liam gently pulled her closer. His gaze lowered to her lips and then back up to her eyes. Barely able to breathe, she nodded. "Truce."

"You have paint all over your face." He reached up and lightly rubbed it off her cheek, his thumb trailing over her jaw.

"So do you." She grinned, watching as he leaned closer.

"I don't mind if you don't."

She gave a slight shake of her head and reached up to pull him down to her. His eyes widened, but as soon as her lips touched his, he pulled her closer, deepening the kiss.

"What in the heavens is going on here?"

And just like that, the spell was broken, and Liam pulled away from her, taking several steps to the side.

"We are painting our lantern, Mother."

"Well, I can see that." A disproving stare floated past her son and landed on Mia. "Perhaps you can actually get a little bit of paint on the lantern this time?"

"Of course."

"The Way of Light Festival is a vital part of your engagement. It's not a game or something to play with."

"You're right. We're sorry, Mother."

"Make sure you get cleaned up after you're finished. It's almost dinnertime." Before she turned to walk away, Mia could have sworn the queen tried to hide a grin and a chuckle. "Because I think we will all be dining together tonight."

Chapter Eighteen

"Your Highness, are you with us?"

"Yes, of course." Liam sat straighter in his chair and ignored the looks of annoyance from the council. Five men, excluding himself and Luka, occupied the long table in the council Room. For weeks now, his father had insisted on Liam taking charge of the meetings to prepare for inheriting the throne. Shortly afterward, the rebels started attacking and stealing their supplies.

The speaker of the group, council Speaker Davis, spoke up. "What has your team learned about these so-called rebels and the food shortage?"

Liam tensed, knowing the question had to come up eventually. "We are very close to learning how they intercept our distribution sites."

An aging bald man beside Liam scoffed. "Which is a fancy way of saying that you are no closer to a positive outcome than you were last week."

"Hector, watch your tone," Davis interrupted before Liam could respond. "I'm sure Prince Liam is doing everything in his power to find these rebels."

"No one thinks that's not the case, Speaker Davis." Another man across from Liam added. "But you can't ignore that this has gone on long enough."

Liam needed to interject before the conversation made a turn. "Gentlemen, I agree with you. No one is more frustrated and upset by this than I am. We have exhausted every avenue in this situation, but these rebels seem to be one step ahead of us every time."

"Your Highness, we've switched up the routes, the drivers, and the delivery dates." Council Speaker Davis sighed and looked around the table before landing his gaze back on him. "I think it's time to acknowledge that someone on the inside is working with the rebels."

Silence filled the council room. Liam leaned back in his chair, thoughts racing. He had feared this very thing for weeks, but with each step along the way, he wanted—needed—to give his people the benefit of the doubt. Why would someone do this to their sector? The people were already suffering. Trade routes were being negotiated with the other sectors that had far better bargaining chips than they had.

"Prince Liam, I know you don't want to admit this, but by this point, we have to assume the worst." Hector tapped the table with his finger. "Since the Tenebrous Era, the sectors have slowly forgotten about the good of the whole and focused on their sole lands. Allies have turned on each other just to get a cheaper price on goods."

His tone grew angrier with each new declaration. "New trade agreements have singled out other sectors, and all the while, the Southern Sector has stuck their heads in the sand and ignored the issues—hoping it would all resolve itself—and now we have rebels trying to feed our country!"

Not a single person at the table made a sound. But every pair of eyes turned to Liam. He took a moment to harness his anger. "The Dunne family has always wanted to hear the opinions of our peers and seek wise counsel, Hector. And while that will not change in my rule, you are dangerously close to getting thrown out of these meetings."

Hector's face turned scarlet.

"We have not hidden our heads in the sand. We are actively seeking these thieves, which is what they are, Hector—thieves. They aren't stealing resources to feed our people but selling it for a higher profit."

"You can't deny we are on the precipice of losing the people's trust."

It wasn't very often that Liam's anger got the best of him, but Hector was a man who liked to push his buttons. Liam had to remind himself not to lose his head. It wouldn't do anything but give Hector more room to argue that he wasn't up to the task of managing the shipping and trading. "I'm well aware—better than anyone here, for that fact—or has my engagement to Princess Amelia escaped your memory?"

Murmurs filled the room, but Speaker Davis spoke up over the noise. "And we all agree that an alliance with the Western Sector in marriage will benefit our sector greatly."

"Speaking of the princess, have you learned why she arrived alone or without identification? Her advisor says all is well, but I think I speak for all of us that there's something not right with the lady. She certainly doesn't act like a princess."

Hector just didn't know when to stop. This man was single-handedly trying to undermine Liam at every turn. He wouldn't have the nerve to do this if the king was in the room.

Liam leveled a glare at the man. "I will not question my fiancée and drudge up the circumstances of her arrival. No doubt they were traumatic for her, and I'm sure she will confide in me when she is ready." He stood to his feet and buttoned his jacket, ready to excuse himself from this sham of a meeting. "And as you pointed out, Hector, Mr. Ortega vouched for her identity."

Davis got to his feet, and the other men joined him, one by

one. "Of course, Your Highness. No one expects you to traumatize the princess further." Sweat beaded along the man's hairline, and he dabbed it with a handkerchief. "I think tensions are high for everyone at the moment, that's all."

"Thank you, Speaker Davis." Liam gave him a brief nod, then nodded to the rest of the men. "Gentlemen, please excuse me. There's somewhere else I need to be." He turned to look at his servant and friend. "Luka."

Luka nodded and followed him out of the room, falling into step beside him in the direction of Liam's private study.

"You handled that well, Your Highness."

"Do you think my father sends me in there as some sort of punishment?"

"I doubt it, Your Highness." Luka laughed. "He's had his share of those meetings himself."

"I can't imagine having to deal with that on a daily basis." He pushed open the door of his study and laid his suit jacket across the back of a chair. "Luka, please have some refreshments brought up to my office, and have Captain Brooks join us. We need to take another look at the soldiers deployed to track the rebels, and I want to investigate our entire distributive team."

"As much as I hate to give them credit, I can't disagree with the council that there must be an inside informant."

"I know. It's been my fear as well." Liam pulled his chair out from behind his desk and sat. "But we've already looked at everyone and didn't come up with any firm evidence."

Luka raised an eyebrow. "I know you don't want to hear this, but perhaps it's time to bring the king in."

Before Liam could protest, Luka held up his hand and continued. "I know he gave this issue over to you, but you've said yourself that the Dunnes always seek wise council. And we can't deny that your father is a wise and knowledgeable king."

Liam rubbed a hand over his face and sighed. It pained him to agree, but he knew Luka was right. His father wasn't a warm and approachable king, but he was smart and good at investigating and strategic planning. He knew he had to bring his father into the situation, but he wished he had some sort of clue or information at hand when he did so.

Liam leaned back in his chair and finally nodded. "All right. Ask my father to join us."

Chapter Nineteen

The brisk early autumn breeze sent a ripple of goosebumps down Luna's arms as she climbed out of the car and picked up speed to match Princess Amelia's stride. "You seem more agitated than usual this morning."

"I'm fine." Amelia kept up her pace down the uneven sidewalk of the marketplace, not in the least worried that Luna was walking beside her instead of behind her, as royal etiquette demanded.

"You really can't fool me, you know. I can see right through you." She hissed but then averted her eyes and fell back half a step as they crossed a merchant pulling out a cart of wares from their shop.

Amelia turned and called over her shoulder. "Luna, what's gotten into you? Can't you keep up?"

"I can't, Your Highness, remember?"

Amelia frowned and then slowed, looking around before crossing over to a display of scarves. "These are so lovely," she told the owner, who flushed in appreciation. "Do you happen to have any in purple?"

"Of course, Your Highness. I'll be right back."

The lady hurried into the shop, and Amelia whispered. "I'm not going to your store today."

"Oh really? And where are you going then?"

"To the chapel."

Luna gasped, not even trying to hide her shock, and hissed. "You can't!" What if someone overheard their conversation? Luna glanced over her shoulder to make sure the guard wasn't too close. Luckily, he was observing the crowd that gathered down the street instead of Princess Amelia. Something must have piqued his interest because he started approaching the group.

Luna let out a long sigh.

"And why not?"

"It's forbidden." Luna barely got the words out before the shopkeeper returned with a dark purple scarf. She handed it to the princess, who grinned, running the fabric through her fingers.

"It's beautiful. I'll take it."

The shopkeeper beamed at them, soaking in the praise from the princess. "Thank you, Princess Amelia. I'll wrap it up for you."

Luna pulled the pouch hanging from her wrist, dug a few coins for the scarf, and exchanged them for a neatly wrapped package.

Amelia left the booth and continued up the street—away from Luna's jewelry shop. What was she going to do? It's not like she could just grab the princess's arm and pull her away. That would draw more attention than the curious onlookers had already sent their way.

Instead, she followed closely behind Amelia, trying to appear relaxed, but inside, a war waged. The closer they came to the chapel, the more panic set in. There had to be something Luna could do. Perhaps she could simply go back and get the guard? But one look in his direction confirmed she wouldn't have time. Plus, there was no way to guarantee that Amelia wouldn't cause a scene.

Too late. They were already close to the chapel's doors. Luna had to make a decision. Perhaps it wouldn't be that bad just to reach out, spin the princess around, and march her back to her shop. Her fingertips grazed Amelia's shoulder.

"You won't stop me, Luna, so don't even try." Amelia pressed on, pushing open the doors of the chapel.

Luna's steps faltered for just a moment before she ducked into the old building and closed the door behind her. She leaned against it, her heart beating wildly in her chest. "We have just a few minutes before the guard returns from the crowd."

"That's all I need." Amelia rushed to the back of the chapel toward the frame of an empty window.

"What are you doing?"

"I'm going home."

Luna pushed herself from the door and stepped forward. Did she hear her correctly?

"There has to be a way to go back." The Princess mumbled under her breath, bending down, feeling along the walls, and sticking her arm through the window. "Maybe it only activates if I jump back through."

"Have you entirely lost it?" Luna shrieked, running to the princess and grabbing around her waist to stop her from climbing through.

The princess fought against her hold, grabbing the wooden frame and stopping Luna from pulling her backward. "Let go, Luna!"

"Everyone can see you! You're going to ruin our cover." Luna took advantage of Amelia's hesitation and yanked her one more time. The princess released her hold of the frame and dropped down to the ground.

"I had to try." Tears filled Amelia's eyes. "I know you don't want details, and I promised I wouldn't say, but Luna, I just want to go home."

"And how will this old, empty frame help you?"

Amelia sighed. "You're right. It's not going to help." She wiped a tear running down her cheek. "I need the actual window.

The stained-glass window." Her eyes brightened, and she pointed to the frame. "Luna, do you know what happened to this window?"

"I have no idea. It's been broken for as long as I can remember. Since the Tenebrous Era."

"Is there anyone who would know?"

Luna shook her head, a frown tugging at her lips. What was so important about the chapel window that she risked getting them both in trouble? Before she could stop herself, she gripped the girl's shoulders, her fingers digging in more than she meant to. "You have to pull it together. You're putting us in danger!"

Amelia's eyes widened, fear flickering across her face.

She eased her grip and sighed. "Look, we need to go. We aren't supposed to be in here."

Amelia must have realized the desperation in her voice because she finally nodded and let Luna walk her down the aisle and back outside. "Come on, we will go to my shop."

The guard met them at the bottom of the stairs, a deep scowl on his face. Amelia just walked past him, avoiding his gaze and holding her chin high. He didn't question them, but by the set of his jaw, he seemed just as worried as Luna.

His gaze never left Princess Amelia as they walked down the sidewalk toward Luna's jewelry shop. She took the time of silence to gather her thoughts and get her racing heart back to a normal rhythm. Surely, this guard wouldn't say anything. Besides, if he did, Luna could argue that he left them on their own for the entire time.

There. At least she had some leverage. They stopped at the shop's door, and she reached in her pocket for her keys. But the guard pulled a tablet from his pocket before she could unlock the door.

"I'm sorry, princess, but you're needed back at the castle."

"*Oh?*" Amelia acted surprised, but Luna couldn't ignore the flash of worry that flickered in her eyes.

"Something about the lantern for the festival."

Amelia gave him a smile and waved her hand. "Prince Liam and I finished that yesterday."

His fingers moved quickly over the buttons on the device, not even bothering to look back at her. Within seconds, a black car pulled up in front of the shop, and another guard climbed out and held the door open.

"You may have finished it, Your Highness, but now it's missing."

Chapter Twenty

There wasn't much time to wipe away the tears from her visit to the chapel, but Mia did her best to rub away the blotchiness under her eyes. Of course, that only made them redder. Luna looked over her hair and smoothed the wayward strands the wind had blown out of place.

Her heart ached. Even though a part of her knew the empty window wouldn't take her home, the other part hoped it would. Now, she had to come to terms with the fact she probably *couldn't* go home. Luna didn't know where the window was, and from the sounds of it, asking about the window wasn't allowed. It was most likely destroyed when the chapel was outlawed.

They exited the car, and instead of going to her room to change out of her dress into something more suitable for daywear at the castle, they passed by the ballroom and headed out to the gardens.

Why would someone steal their lantern? The Way of Light Festival was merely hours away, and she and the prince had to devise a suitable replacement. She relaxed her face and plastered on what she hoped was a pleasant smile. Mia had to push away the sadness of the missing window and focus on the task at hand.

Getting through the Way of Light Festival. She was back to

pretending. As much as she hated it, there wasn't another option or time to come up with another way out. For now, she was Princess Amelia.

Prince Liam rose to his feet as she approached the table. Another lantern was set in the center of the table with the same paints from the day before.

"Princess Amelia, thank you for coming back so quickly."

"Well, we can't show up at the festival without the main attraction." She gave him a playful smile and grabbed a freshly laundered apron draped across the chair.

"You're right. But maybe we hold off on the paint fight this time?"

Face heating at the thought of their shared kiss and how she was the one who initiated it, she slipped the apron over her head and held out the straps for Luna to tie. "Yes, I think that's probably a good idea."

They settled into the routine of painting the lantern and stenciling on a scrolled design along the bottom edges, finishing it with their initials on each side.

"Do you remember what wish you had placed inside the lantern?" Prince Liam asked, picking up a piece of paper and handing her one.

"I do." She took a seat at the table and picked up a pen. "But do you think we should discuss them first?" What made her ask that? She nibbled on her lip, unsure if it was even a good idea to talk about their joint vision of the sector because there wouldn't be a wedding. She planned to be long gone before then.

Liam leaned back in his seat and thoughtfully nodded. "I think that's a great idea. I will be king, but you will be equally important to the kingdom, to the people—to me." He stumbled over the last addition and looked away. "Well—one day. I know this isn't what either of us may have envisioned for our lives."

"No, I suppose it's not." She cleared the tears from her throat, his kind words twisting in her gut. "But I think we've made a good team so far." It was the truth but empty of promises. She wouldn't do that to him. It would only end up hurting them both.

Liam clapped his hands and then picked up his pen. "Okay, well, let's do this. I know Luna must be chomping at the bit to get you ready for tonight."

At the mention of Luna's name, she looked around the garden but couldn't find the girl. How odd. She usually kept a close presence. "I'm sure she is, but I do not know where she went."

"I'm sure she's not far."

Something wasn't quite right. Mia couldn't explain the feeling or why, but she suddenly feared for her maid. Perhaps it was merely the fact that Luna was the one who put the lantern up last night. But she wouldn't go so far as taking it—that Mia knew for a fact. Luna had as many reasons for getting through these festivals as she did.

"Princess Amelia?"

At the sound of Liam's voice, she turned back in her chair. "Yes, sorry. Where were we?"

He raised an eyebrow but didn't press her further. "We were writing our wishes."

"How about you start?" She placed the pen on the table and wiped her palms on her apron, unsure what to suggest. Yesterday, she put something generic, but now, that didn't seem like it was enough.

"I suppose, like any fair ruler, I want my people to prosper and to be happy." His brow furrowed as if there was more he wanted to say.

"What is it?"

"I'm not going to lie to you, Princess Amelia. As you know, our union will naturally benefit both sectors." His voice lowered, and she had to lean forward to hear him better. "But especially mine. My people are going hungry, and we haven't been able to stop it."

Before she could think better of it, she reached out and placed her hand on his. "Oh, Liam, I'm so sorry."

His eyes widened, and she realized her mistake. She called him by his first name. "Forgive me, Your Highness."

She started to pull her hand away, but he gently held it, rubbing his thumb across the top. "There's no need to apologize. I think we can move past formal titles. What do you think?"

She nodded, caught up in the sincerity of his words. "In that case, call me Mia." A tiny bit of happiness worked its way into her heart at the idea of him using her real name. "It's what my close friends and family call me."

"Mia?" He gave her a grin. "I like that. It suits you."

The garden doors opened, banging against the castle wall with such a force that Mia startled, jerking her hand away from Liam's as he hastily stood.

A tall, imposing man with wide shoulders walked toward them, a scowl on his face. "What did I hear about the lantern being stolen?"

"There seems to have been a slight hiccup, but it's since been remedied." Liam gestured to the new lantern on the table. "Princess Amelia and I have finished a replacement one."

"Well ... that's good then." The man relaxed his posture and nodded. "I just wanted to make sure everything went smoothly for tonight."

"Of course, Mr. Ortega. We all want tonight to be perfect."

Mia stiffened at the name. The advisor for Western Sector— Princess Amelia's advisor. What was she going to do now? Miraculously, she had managed to stay away from the man, but now, he would take one look at her and know the truth.

"Forgive me for interrupting. I will see you both tonight." The advisor gave Liam a quick bow and then turned to her. "Princess Amelia, if you need anything, just let me know."

Did he just threaten her? His back was to Liam, so he couldn't see anything, but she could. His gaze was hard and cold. Nowhere even close to the kindness as his words and tone sounded. Yes, that was indeed a threatening look. He *wanted* her to play the part of the princess. But why?

She shakily got to her feet and nodded. "Thank you, Mr. Ortega."

With that, he turned on his heel and left, passing by Luna, who was making her way down the path to them. As Luna came closer, Mia noticed how red and blotchy her eyes were. She was right. Something happened. She reached for her maid's arm and drew her in.

"Luna, are you all right?"

"I'm fine, Princess Amelia."

"Did you get in trouble for the lantern?"

"A scolding, but I didn't take the lantern, Your Highness."

Angry, Mia sighed. "I know you didn't. Who scolded you?"

Luna shifted her eyes toward Liam, who was back to writing on his slip of paper.

"It's not important. But what is, though, is that you must get ready for the party."

"You're right. It's getting late, isn't it?" She walked over to Liam and briefly touched his arm to get his attention. "Liam, I have to get ready for the festival, but I'll see you in a little while?"

"Of course." He gave her a grin. "I'll finish the wish and place it in the lantern."

It wasn't until she was halfway back to her suite that she remembered that she never shared her wish for the lantern with him. Luckily, he didn't seem to mind, so perhaps she could just share his wish. How could she come up with a wish for the sector she didn't plan on staying in much longer?

Chapter Twenty-One

The Marketplace was packed. Prince Liam had never seen so many people lining the streets or between the buildings surrounding the entrance to the park. Palace servants had strung twinkling white lights down the path to the gazebo and along the structure's roof where the Way of Light Festival would take place.

Refreshment tables with white linens graced the right side of the park, and Liam wondered how much that dipped into the castle's pantry. He didn't mind, though. Not when it meant his people would have a little extra food tonight.

"What's that smile for?"

Mia walked up the gazebo steps and took her place beside him. Blonde curls fell past her shoulders, tied back with a single blue ribbon. He had the sudden urge to cup her cheek and kiss her again. "I was just admiring the view."

Her mouth opened, shock widening her eyes before she recovered. "Well, you're right. These stars are beautiful."

What was wrong with him? *Get ahold of yourself, Liam.* He cleared his throat and changed topics. "Did you know that this town was once called Park Haven?" He whispered, leaning in close to her ear. "My ancestors settled here hundreds of years ago from Ireland." He gestured to the crowd, conversing and eating around them. "There's something beautiful about seeing everyone together, from the poor, working class, all the way to the courtiers mingling together under one open sky."

"That's something to be proud of, Liam. To remember where you came from and where you want to go. Your people are blessed to have you."

Blessed.

He hadn't thought of that word in a long time, but Princess Amelia had a way of recalling the old ways back to him. His heritage, God's legacy. He wanted that to be a guiding light for his people. But there were so many laws hindering that from happening.

"Did I say something to upset you?" Her voice was low, but he could still hear the worry in her words.

"No, of course not. You just challenge my thinking, Mia." He reached for her hand and looped his fingers through hers. "And that's a good thing."

All uncertainty left her eyes at his declaration, and Liam held her gaze. A person could get lost in the depths of her eyes, and the more he stared, the longer he wanted to.

A figure stepped into his peripheral, forcing him to break off the connection with Mia. "*Ah*, Mother. You look stunning." Still holding Mia's hand, he used his free one and gently embraced his mother, her face lighting up at the praise.

"And you, my dear boy, look ... content." She pulled back from his hug but still held on to his arm, turning her attention to Mia. "Princess Amelia, how are you tonight?"

Mia curtsied, her hair falling over her shoulder. "I'm well. Thank you for asking, Your Majesty. And you?"

A flicker of a grin tugged at Mother's lips before she answered. "If I can pull the king away from the dessert table long enough to start the festivities officially, then I will be right as rain."

Liam searched the gazebo until he found his father holding a plate of cake. A group of courtiers was talking to him—their faces serious. "It might be easier for you to start it yourself."

Mother followed his gaze and sighed. "I'm afraid you may be right. Both of you follow me over to the podium."

Nodding, he pulled Mia's hand up and tucked it into the crook of his arm. "Lead the way."

Walking behind his mother, they stopped several times as nearby subjects bowed and then moved out of their way. With each stop, his mother was gracious, taking the time to greet each guest and talk for a moment with them.

"That must become exhausting," Mia whispered, still holding onto his arm.

"It can, at times, for sure." He answered, matching her tone. "But I'm sure you've experienced that in your sector."

"Of course ... I just meant ..."

"That it can become overwhelming?"

"Exactly."

"Well, if anyone can make it look easy, my mother can." Liam got into place behind the queen at the lectern, gently pulling Mia beside him. "I'm not sure how she does it."

"May I have everyone's attention, please?" The Queen announced into the microphone and waited until a hush fell over the crowd. "Thank you so much for joining us tonight to celebrate Prince Liam and Princess Amelia's engagement."

The crowd applauded, and Mia's fingers gripped his arm tighter. "You're going to do the talking, correct?"

"I can." Taking a closer look at Mia's face, he noticed the fear in her eyes as the crowd gathered closer. This wasn't the first time he witnessed that specific look on her face or observed her body language change from confident to nervous. Before, he had assumed it was because she was in a new place, but now, he could tell it had gone much deeper.

Was Princess Amelia scared to speak in public?

Speaking and being in the public eye was a normal, everyday part of a royal. He learned how to act in public and give speeches from his tutor at a very young age. His parents never hid him from view and insisted that the best way for him to learn was by standing at their side at court.

Did Mia's parents not do the same? Was that why she was so uncomfortable? Liam never stopped to think about how hard the crowds would be if one feared them.

The more time he spent with her, the more their differences presented themselves, but it made him want to get to know her even more.

As the cheering died down, he forced himself back to his mother's speech.

"The Way of Light Festival is a treasured tradition we are proud to witness tonight. I remember my own with such fondness and love—as it has become one of my most favorite memories."

His mother gestured to the table beside the lectern. "Each royal couple is asked to create a lantern together and write upon it their wishes for their people during their union and reign."

The queen beckoned Liam and Mia to step forward, a radiant smile on her face. "And I'm proud to introduce Prince Liam and Princess Amelia's lantern to you tonight."

The crowd cheered louder as Liam stepped up to the microphone, and his mother moved to the side.

He gently lowered Mia's hand and reached for the notes that someone—no doubt Luka—had already placed on the lectern for him.

"Thank you, Mother, for your beautiful and kind words." He leaned toward the microphone, smoothing the pages in front of him. "When Princess Amelia and I met to make our lantern, I had already had my wish in my mind." He looked over at Mia and grinned. "But then, this wonderful woman beside me reminded me that we should discuss our wishes together. And she was right. These wishes are more than just well-meaning words. They are our vision for our sector. For our people."

A few whistles filled the air, followed quickly with polite

clapping. "Our vision for you is that the Southern Kingdom will flourish, prosper, and be blessed. That together, as one people, we will look back on our past and remember where we came from. That we will honor what we've done and who came before us. But we will also look toward the future with hope of who we will become. That we will learn from our past and use it to make our future the best it can be."

This time, the applause was genuine. The people had heard his words and knew it came from his heart. He looked back at Mia, who gave him a nod of approval. "We are proud to present you with our lantern." He picked up a match from the table and passed it to Mia, and then picked up one for himself. Once at the bottom of the stairs, they lit the inside of the lantern together and lifted it up. The crowd *oohed* and *aahed* as the lantern rose in the night sky toward the stars.

"That was beautiful." Mia wrapped an arm around his waist, leaning in as they watched the lantern slowly drift away.

"It was all you. I just listened and took notes."

"Your people adore you." She gestured around as the band resumed their place, and music filled the park once more. The crowd thinned out, some dancing, some returning to the food tables, and some still hovering around the podium. "And it's not hard to see why."

Her face reddened at her revelation, and his pulse quickened, the urge to lean down and kiss her overwhelming him once more. She must have been embarrassed, though, because she averted her eyes. So, he pulled her close and gently placed a kiss on the side of her temple. "I think they will come to adore you too—I know I have."

Chapter Twenty-Two

"I think they make a good couple."

Luna forced her gaze from her lap to the patio table where Prince Liam and Princess Amelia were enjoying lunch. "I suppose so."

Her father frowned, turning his parental stare in her direction. "Luna, is everything all right?"

She wiped her palms on her apron. "Of course. Why?"

"The Way of Light Festival was days ago, and you seem ... distracted."

Leave it to her father to see straight through her and to the heart of the matter. In her twenty-three years of life, she'd never been able to hide anything from him. Why she thought she could now, she had no idea. "Perhaps I am," Luna sighed. "It's just—"

"You miss your store."

Shocked, Luna slowly nodded. She almost slipped up and confessed everything to her father. Instead, she sighed in relief. "Yes."

It wasn't a lie. She missed her quaint brick building in the marketplace and her small apartment above it. But more than that, she missed overseeing her own schedule. Of answering only to herself.

"I'm sorry, Luna. I didn't mean to rip you away from your livelihood." Regret filled his tone. "When Prince Liam asked me, I didn't stop to think what that meant for you."

"You don't have to apologize, Father." Luna squeezed his arm. "It's not like you or I could have said no. Besides, I think I've seen more of you here at the castle than when I was at my shop."

"True." He reached over and laid his hand on top of hers. "I've enjoyed seeing you here too. But I'm sure it won't be long before they hire another maid to take your place."

Giving her dad a nod and a fake grin, she pulled her hand away and placed it in her lap. Another maid? What would Mia do if another girl took her place? And what would Mr. Ortega do if he found out they replaced her? No doubt he would count that as a failure on her part and take it out on her father.

A shudder ran across her shoulders and down her arms. She'd experienced firsthand how violent the advisor from the Western Sector could be. She still had bruises on her arms to prove it.

Stealing a peek at her father, she watched as he finished the last of his lunch. Every couple of bites, his eyes would train back on Prince Liam and then around the garden. Everything about her father boasted pride in being Liam's most trusted advisor. He'd based his whole life on teaching, molding, and guiding Prince Liam. His voice oozed with pride and love when he spoke about him.

No one could do a better job in his shoes. And everyone knew it. The sector was far better off having her father work for the crown. She would never let anyone jeopardize his position—or his life.

Because if they replaced her, her mission would fail, and her father's life would come to a halt. She wouldn't let that happen.

Panic settled in her stomach, churning her grilled chicken and mashed potatoes into an unpleasant concoction.

"Father!" Her voice tittered on the edge of hysterical, so she cleared her throat and tried again. "Father, I think it would be best if I stay on with Princess Amelia until after the ceremonies."

"*Oh*, is that right?" He wiped his mouth with the linen napkin and returned it to his lap. "I just assumed you were ready to go home."

"The shop will still be there when I get back, and I really think that it would be beneficial for Princess Amelia to have the same maid throughout all of this. As you can imagine, it's a big change, and we've settled into a nice routine. I wouldn't want to upset her by even more change."

"You, my daughter, are so kind to think of her." He gave her a small grin. "Just like your mother."

A ping of sadness stabbed her at the mention of her mother, but she stuffed down the feelings and flippantly said, "Well, if you say so."

"In many ways, you are the spitting image of your mother. You have her eyes and her smile. But don't ever forget that while you have her looks, you also have something even better."

Tears glistened in his eyes, and Luna regretted her teasing tone. "You are kind and brave. Determined. Those are all her qualities as well, and I see them grow in you each day."

"I wish she was here. That I had the opportunity to grow up with her."

"My sweet, I wish that every day." He sniffed, stacking dishes together. "But she knew you. Even if it was for a few hours, and she was so proud. Never forget that."

"Did she want me to become a lady's maid like her?"

Father's hand froze in midair for a moment as if he was thinking of the right thing to say. Finally, he shook his head. "She wanted whatever path was meant for you. She loved serving the queen but loved you even more and would never stifle God's path for you."

Luna looked around the garden, relieved to find it empty. She leaned across the table and hissed. "Father, you must be careful. Such talk is forbidden, and you know it." Tears pricked the corners of her eyes. "If someone heard you—"

"I know, my sweet, I know." He wiped his brow. "I'm sorry.

When I think of your mother—she never wanted us to hide who we are."

"We aren't in the Western Sector where there are secret followers, Father. We are in the South. Where even a whisper of His name means imprisonment."

"There was a time before the Tenebrous Era that the South was in what they called the ..." His words cut off, but he mouthed the next ones, "*Bible Belt*." He narrowed his eyes, his jaw tensing. "I bet those people would be heartbroken and ashamed to see what has become of their country."

"I'm sure they would, Father, but we live in *this* country. Right *now*. So, we must always be on guard, even if we don't like it."

He had always taught her these very things. So, why was he suddenly risking this discussion in the open?

"You're right, and I'll be more careful." Standing up, he adjusted his uniform jacket. "But I hear you about Princess Amelia. Perhaps it would be better all-around for you to stay. To help things go smoothly. I've noticed she tends to become overwhelmed easily."

Luna stood. "Yes, she does."

Father studied her for a moment as if he were waiting for her to elaborate, but when she didn't, he finally nodded. "Okay, I will speak to the prince and see if I can get him to wait on your replacement. No guarantees he will do so, though."

"Thank you, Father." She walked around the table and wrapped her arms around his waist. "You really are the best."

"Well, that's easy when I have you." He let go and glanced at his watch. "Now, I have a few more minutes, so tell me about what happened with the lantern. I know you didn't take it."

Irritation flooded her, and it was the last thing she wanted to talk about. "Honestly, I'm not sure who did. But I get the feeling it was some sort of prank."

"Who would want to do that?"

She raised an eyebrow. "Come on, Father. I'm not exactly Miss Popularity here."

"What do you mean?"

"The other maids. I kind of swooped in and stole their promotion. One that several felt should have been given to them instead of someone who doesn't even live in the castle."

"I see." He frowned. "I'm sorry. That thought never even crossed my mind when I asked you to come."

"It's just castle politics." Luna sneered. "The whole reason I wanted out to begin with." *Uh-oh*, she had to be careful, or she would undo all her persuasiveness to stay in the palace as Amelia's maid. She waved her hand in dismissal. "But please don't worry. It's not a big deal. It won't be long, and these girls will move on to something else to gripe about."

Whether or not he believed her, he didn't say. Instead, he just nodded. "Well, kiddo, lunch is over, and it's back to work." He kissed her forehead. "I'll see you later."

She nodded and followed behind him as they made their way to the royal couple. Amelia's afternoon was booked solid with preparation for the next ceremony, and somehow in there, she had to find time to sneak away with her for their next princess lesson and discuss the detour to the chapel.

This whole thing had become much more involved than she originally thought. The lies just continued to stack on top of each other. How long would it be before they all came crashing down?

Chapter Twenty-Three

"Are you sure we can talk freely in here?" Mia pulled a chair from the art studio window and placed it at a small round table in the center of the room.

"We can't keep going to my shop, or someone will start questioning it." Luna tapped her fingers on the table. "This is the only place I can think of that won't raise suspicion."

"Okay, so what am I supposed to learn today?"

"Today is all about the Western Sector." Luna got to her feet and pulled a notebook out of a bag in the center of the table. "I was only a kid when my father and I left there, so I don't remember much. But I did some digging in the library and came up with as much information as possible."

Mia set up, folding her arms on the table. "Spill it."

Luna leaned back. "What?"

"It just means to tell me, that I'm ready to listen."

Her maid's eyebrow raised in question, but then she shook her head and continued. "Princess Amelia Elizabeth Lockridge was born in 2151—"

"2151!" Mia clamped her hand over her mouth after she realized she shrieked. Forcing herself to calm down, she quietly added. "And how old is she?"

"Twenty-two," Luna said softly, her face pale. She leaned back in her chair as if trying to decide what to say next.

"So, the year is 2173?"

"Yes. One hundred years since the Tenebrous Era."

The air in the room grew stale, and for a brief few seconds, it seemed as if Mia would suffocate. She pushed back from the table and reached for a nearby notepad. She fanned her face and paced back and forth along the enormous windows. She had traveled one hundred and fifty years into the future.

One hundred and fifty years!

Black spots speckled her vision, and Mia bent over, placing her hands on her knees. One hundred and fifty years. The more she thought about it, the more insane it sounded.

"You're starting to scare me. Mia, what is happening?"

She waved a hand in Luna's direction. "I'm just a little freaked out myself. Are you sure it's 2173?"

"I wouldn't lie about the year, Mia."

Her breath became shallow, and a sharp pain hit her squarely in the chest. "I'm never going home."

The realization hit her so hard that she nearly fell to the floor. It had always been in the back of her mind since she'd arrived, but going back to the chapel the other day and now, learning just how far in the future she'd come, had clinched it.

Mia was stuck in the year 2173.

She had to sit down before she passed out. She fumbled her way to the chair and collapsed on it.

"Are you all right?" Luna touched the back of Mia's forehead with her hand. "You don't have a fever."

"No. I don't think I will be all right ever again." She managed to squeak out in between shallow breaths and tears.

Luna's eyes widened, but she jumped into action, filling a glass with water and placing it in her hand. "Drink."

Inhaling, Mia took deep breaths through her nose and let them out through her mouth as she slowly sipped the water.

Luna went to the sink and dampened a clean cloth. "Here, put this on the back of your neck. Maybe that will help."

"Thank you."

"You're welcome, and you don't mean that, you know," Cold hands gripped hers, and Mia looked down to see that Luna had kneeled in front of her. "Everything will be all right. Because we are going to get through this together."

Whether it was the cool rag on her neck or Luna's icy hands, the chill jolted her nervous system back into proper order. The pressure in her chest relaxed, but it didn't take away the anguish in her heart. Grief for her sister and her home overtook her, and she cried.

Luna wrapped her in a hug, which brought on more tears. She didn't try to reassure Mia, or shush her, but just held on and let her cry until she was spent.

Finally, she pulled away. "Luna, I know you said you didn't want details, but—"

"I think we are past details now. Our last conversation and this breakdown are enough proof." Luna gave her a sympathetic smile. "I think we both need to know everything."

Nodding, Mia took in a steadying breath and let it out slowly. "I tried to tell you before, but I got too afraid to elaborate."

There was nothing else to lose. She knew in her heart she wouldn't find that window to go home. If she told her maid the truth and it backfired, maybe it would make it easier to leave the castle and try to start a new life somewhere.

"Luna, I'm from the year 2023."

It was her maid's turn to react. She withdrew her hands and sat back, all the color draining from her cheeks. She shook her head in denial. "That's not possible."

"Believe me, I've been telling myself that every day since I arrived."

Luna stared at her, her mouth slightly hanging open. "But that's before the Tenebrous Era."

Mia nodded. "*Fifty years* before, if I did the math correctly."

"This is unbelievable." Luna scrambled to her feet. Was she having a panic attack, too, now?

"No wonder you know nothing." She turned back with an apologetic look. "I'm sorry, that came out wrong."

"It's fine. I know what you meant."

Luna started pacing again. "Okay, so that's why you're obsessed with the chapel and that empty window frame."

"It was my sister's wedding day when I fell through the stained-glass window and landed in your broken-down chapel."

"You were in the Southern Sector's chapel in 2023?" Luna came back around the table and sat beside her. "Wow."

"Well, Park Haven's Chapel. Yes, I was there, and I didn't even get to say goodbye to my sister, June." Her throat tightened. "But it doesn't matter now because the window's gone, and I can't go home."

"No wonder you've been so anxious. I thought you were just really afraid of everything."

"I've always had anxiety, but being in a whole new world has not helped."

"Okay, so obviously, I can't dispute what you're saying. I mean, I have no proof. It's completely unbelievable, but why would you tell me a blatant lie?" Luna seemed to be working out her thoughts out loud, so Mia stayed silent and let her ramble.

Luna jumped up again and moved over to the windows, keeping her back to Mia. "You show up dressed like you're from the Western Sector, but that's where the similarities stop. You don't act, talk, or carry yourself like a princess—or someone from this time, really." She massaged her temples. "Either I'm losing my mind, or you're telling me the truth."

Mia waited as Luna stared out the window, mumbling something else she couldn't hear. She would let her have all the time she needed to come to terms with what Mia had told her. Except Mia had had weeks to wrap her head around it, and she still couldn't.

After what seemed like hours, Luna turned around and

nodded. "Okay, we have our work cut out for us." Her face was all business as she came back to the table and sat across from her. "I'm going to turn you into a princess. One *from* the Western Sector."

Mia bit her lip, afraid to voice the one question that she desperately needed to know the answer to. "So, you believe me, then?"

It took Luna a long time to answer, and Mia was about to give up hope when the girl said, "I don't know what to believe anymore." Her gaze softened, yet resolve lingered in her eyes. "But we are going to get through this together. That I promise."

Chapter Twenty-Four

The exasperated look on Captain Brook's face mimicked the turmoil roiling around inside Prince Liam's stomach. The early morning sun beat down on him, drenching the collar of his shirt. If one more person told him they didn't know how another shipment was stolen ... He kicked a rock and sent it sailing.

"I'm sorry, Your Highness. We aren't sure—"

"Don't finish that sentence," Liam hissed at the guard. "The time for excuses has passed. You promised me extra security measures would be taken and that this wouldn't happen again."

The guard's face paled. "I assure you, Your Highness, that every measure was taken and then some."

"So, can you explain how all we have left is one box of potatoes?" He pounded his fist on top of the box, and it crumpled. "One box!"

"We are reviewing the footage now and hope to have an answer within the hour." The man stumbled over his words and looked away.

"What aren't you saying, Captain Brooks?"

"You know our technology isn't the most ... up to date. It's possible that we ..."

Liam already knew what the man was hesitant to admit. "That we won't be able to tell anything."

"Yes, Your Highness." He bowed his head. "I'm truly sorry. If we had better signal and equipment—"

"I know." Liam sighed, cutting the captain off. "That is not your fault." He pinched the bridge of his nose, trying to gather his racing thoughts and get them in order. The security video wouldn't show who was behind these blatant robberies. The simple fact was their sector was too poor to even acquire the proper equipment. Since the Tenebrous Era, each Kingdom traded resources, and the ones with the most benefitted the most in return. But the Southern Sector was too destroyed by the war and the earthquake to bounce back. And without the means to restore their trade routes back to their former glory, the other sectors took advantage.

"Do you believe your intel was incorrect?" Liam was afraid he already knew the answer to that question. Even so, he wanted to hear it from the captain.

"No, Your Highness. Everything happened as I told you. We intercepted a message from the rebels, left a reply, and fed them a false date and time." Captain Brooks shifted his weight from one leg to another. "Naturally, we had a whole other shipment date in mind. But we didn't make it half a mile down the road before we hit a roadblock with armed men in masks."

"How many people knew of this change in dates?"

"Three, Your Highness—me included."

Dread filled his stomach at the confession. Liam didn't like what he had to do, and from the tone of Captain Brooks, he knew what would happen as well. He eyed the captain, hoping the older man wouldn't hold it against him. "Captain Brooks—"

"Don't worry, Your Highness. I will have the two other men arrested, and then I will turn myself in while you assume command and schedule a trial."

"You have served my family for years. Please don't think for an instant that I believe you've had anything to do with this."

The man nodded. "Your faith in me means the world. But we have a mole, and he must be dealt with. Our people deserve for these rebels to be brought to justice."

Liam reached for the man's shoulder and gave it a squeeze. "You're a good man, Captain Brooks. And an outstanding leader."

Captain Brooks saluted and walked back to his troops, shouting commands for them to load back into the convoy and drive to the castle.

After a few minutes, Liam followed, the weight of his new role settling heavily on his shoulders. He stopped at the truck in the back of the procession, Luka waiting for him beside it.

"Tell me you heard that conversation, for I don't have the heart to repeat it."

Luka opened the door and frowned. "Bits and pieces, Your Highness, but I think I heard the gist."

"Good." He climbed into the backseat and waited while Luka walked around the vehicle and sat beside him. "We have a lot of work to do."

"More hunting, Your Highness?" Apprehension lined his words, bringing a brief smile to his lips. Luka had never enjoyed hunting as much as Liam did.

"Yes, but not the way you're thinking."

"Forgive me, sir. But what are you implying?"

"The rebels, Luka." He turned toward his window and watched the convoy pull onto the road. "It's time to hunt them down."

Chapter Twenty-Five

"Again."

Mia grimaced but did as Luna instructed. The heels clacked against the wooden floor of her sitting room as she walked across it, turned, and walked back toward Luna.

This was ridiculous. Didn't she show up wearing high heels? Of course, she was holding them in her hand, but that was beside the point. She could wear them. So, why go through all of this?

"I don't understand how this will help me become a princess."

"Queens and princesses wear heels occasionally, Mia." Luna sat on the edge of the settee, a disapproving look on her face. "And you, my friend, I'm sorry to say, need some extra practice in that area."

Mia whirled around and glowered at the young woman. "You've gotten a little relaxed in your attitude since you learned my identity the other day."

Luna's eyes widened. "Well done, *Your Highness*. I almost believed that uppity tone."

Mia squelched the urge to roll her eyes. "Is Princess Amelia Lockridge really a snob?"

"I don't know." Luna sighed. "But the Western Sector is not

known for hospitality and warmth. They deal in luxury, wealth, and the best that money and trade goods can buy."

"Doesn't sound like people are that much different here than from my time."

"How do you think the war of the Tenebrous Era happened?" Luna raised an eyebrow. "People have let greed get the best of them throughout history. But not everyone in the Western Sector, or the other ones, for that matter, are all about greed."

"Well, my version of Princess Amelia is not unkind or greedy." Mia kicked off the heels. "And she doesn't like to wear heels."

"Fair enough." Luna giggled and got to her feet. "But there are still royal protocols you must adhere to."

"I know." Mia reached for her flats and slipped them on, ticking the items off on her fingers. "Servants and maids walk behind me. I can't dress myself, fix my hair, serve my food." Mia reached for her class of iced tea and took a drink. "Basically, I'm waited on hand and foot."

"There's so much more to it than that, Mia."

"I'm sure you're right, and I'm sorry. I'm not trying to sound ungrateful for your help." She wiped moisture from the side of her glass. "I just keep thinking that any time I'm going to wake up and be back at home, in my time, where everything makes sense. Where I'm a normal person."

Luna grabbed a plate from the table and filled it with an array of fruit and cheese and passed it over to Mia. She accepted it and watched as Luna fixed another one. "Can you tell me a little bit of what it's like where you're from?"

"Well, technology is at our fingertips, for one. Everyone has cell phones and computers." She grinned at Luna. "And royalty only happens in other countries, not in America."

"What piece of technology do you miss the most?" Luna asked, leaning forward, excitement filling her voice.

"My phone. I miss calling or texting my sister whenever I want to. Also, if I didn't know the answer to something, I could just look it up online." She popped a grape into her mouth. "*Oh!* And watching movies on television."

"We studied your time period in school, you know, but I just can't imagine it."

"Oh, really? Why?"

"Well, because you came right before the Tenebrous Era. We have some of the things you had, but when the Tenebrous Era happened, it wreaked such havoc on society that we never recovered and moved forward."

Luna sighed. "I suppose the leaders who rose after the war didn't want to repeat past mistakes. So, some things stayed the same, like medicine. And some went away, like the internet at everyone's fingertips. But nothing ever progressed back to what it once was."

"What is really going on with the Southern Sector?" Mia bit her lip, unsure if it was her place to ask, but as Princess Amelia, wouldn't she already have some indication of what was going on?

"What do you mean?"

"Prince Liam said that the people are starving, and our engagement is supposed to help?"

"It's true." Luna got up from her seat and poured herself a glass of tea. "The Western Sector, as I said earlier, is extremely wealthy. But they are so because of the food they grow and the coast. They can make deals with the other sectors that we can't."

Mia nodded, unable to wrap her mind around all the talk about trade deals. That's what her engagement was to Liam? A trade deal? While she understood how they operated here, it still left a sour taste in her mouth.

What about love? She mentally shook herself. Mia couldn't afford to think about love right now. She had a part to play—one she was learning was much more important than originally thought. "So, our engagement will help the Southern Sector to have more food?"

"That and better shipping prices." Luna set her drink down and leaned forward. "But there are also the rebels."

"Rebels?"

"I've heard the other servants talk about how a group of people are attacking our soldiers as they bring food supplies to the warehouse."

"That's terrible. Why would they do that?"

Luna shrugged. "Your guess is as good as mine."

Mia finished eating and set the plate on the table in front of her. "If food supplies are so limited, why doesn't the Southern Sector grow their own food?"

"We do as much as we can, but after the war, the land was plagued with environmental disasters. Parts of the country were literally cut off from each other. Large fissures created gaps in the ground, making traveling impossible. With the decay of technology, everything was divided into sectors. Some, of course, fared better than others."

"You mean, like, fault lines? Earthquakes?" Mia's brain raced with the information. Luna must be referring to the New Madrid Fault Line. She shuddered. Growing up, she knew what could happen if it ruptured again, but she never thought it would.

"Exactly. We were far enough away not to be directly hit, but other surrounding states were not so lucky. And our soil has been affected in the years since."

Mia nodded, putting all the pieces together. "Which complicates farming. And if you don't have the funds to fix the trade routes—"

"Exactly."

The grandfather clock chimed, and Mia groaned. "It's already time to get ready for dinner?"

"What's wrong? You're not hungry?" Luna got up from the settee and started for the bedroom. "I know we just had a snack, but dinner's not for another hour or two."

"It's not that. I'm afraid I will slip up, and Liam's parents will know I'm an imposter." She followed her friend to the bedroom and watched as Luna searched through the wardrobe for a suitable dinner dress.

"Look, I was just teasing you earlier, but you are doing a great job." She held up a light blue dress. "And besides, I think Prince Liam is smitten with you."

Her stomach fluttered at the thought. "Funny."

"No, I'm serious. Even my father commented on what a delightful couple you make."

Mia waited as Luna unbuttoned her day dress and helped her slide out of it and into the evening dress. Even if the prince liked her, it didn't change anything. "I'm not Princess Amelia, you know. I'm just Mia. And I hate lying to him."

The azure velvet material felt cool against her skin, and she ran her fingers over it, enjoying how it made her look more regal, even if she didn't feel it.

"I don't like it either." Luna's voice was quiet. "It goes against everything I believe."

"Then why are we? Maybe Liam would help secure me a maid's position, or I could work with you. We could expand your shop." Excitement grew at the idea of using her talents in that way. If she had to start over here, creating and selling her art was the most appealing.

Hands spun her around, and fear radiated from Luna's eyes. She gripped Mia's shoulders, her tone pleading. "Please, Mia. Do not give up now."

"Luna, you're scaring me. What don't I know?"

The maid's eyes glistened. "It's a crime to impersonate a royal."

Mia's stomach roiled. Whatever it was, it must be bad, or Luna wouldn't be warning her. Did she really believe Liam and the others would just let her leave without another word? That she could blend in with the merchants and start a new life?

Still, a part of her didn't want to believe any of it. Liam was kind and understanding. "Do you really think Liam would hurt me?"

Luna let go of her shoulders and sighed. "No, but sometimes a person's station in life doesn't give him a choice."

Chapter Twenty-Six

The door to Liam's office burst open and banged against the wall. "You want to explain why my Captain of the Guard is sitting in a jail cell?"

Liam stood and gestured to the chair in front of his desk. "Good morning, Father, please come in."

"Don't get smart with me, boy." The vein in his father's neck bulged. "Explain. Now."

"The rebels stole another shipment—one that only Captain Brooks and a few other men knew about. I've assumed command until everything can be sorted out."

"Captain Brooks has faithfully served the crown for years."

"Believe me, I am well aware."

"Loyalty means something to the Dunnes." The king narrowed his eyes. "What proof do you have that it was Brooks?"

"I don't—but he insisted." Guilt plagued Liam. He tossed and turned all night because of it. "Father, I don't believe Brooks is our mole, but we can't afford another shipment to be stolen."

His father considered his words and then sat in the chair. His anger slowly dissolved. "How bad is it, really? I know I've let you have the reins on this one, son—but I can tell you haven't told me everything."

"I'm sorry, Father. I thought I could catch the rebels before I needed to worry you more." Liam sat behind his desk and shuffled through the files on top. "I've been supplementing food reserves by sending out hunting parties." Father accepted the files and raised his eyebrow.

"I've even gone myself on some. We've rationed the supplies sold to the markets and restaurants."

"And?"

"It's not enough. Based on inventory at warehouses and shared projections, unless we stop these raids, we will run out of food in a few months."

Father's eyes snapped up from the papers. "So soon?"

"The rebels have intercepted too many convoys, and once we set the limitations in place, the courtiers and merchants panicked and started stockpiling. Causing our poorest not to be able to find even the most basic items."

"The fear of hunger will do that."

"Yes, and I don't blame them, but if we can't find these rebels and bring them to justice—"

"Then fear will ensue, and who knows what will happen next?"

Silence filled the space between them as his father read over the reports. The anger might have gone from his tone and words, but Liam couldn't ignore the disappointment in his father's eyes. Liam never dreamed it would take this long to find the ones responsible and fix the situation before it escalated to this.

He even agreed to marry Princess Amelia to help the kingdom!

"Secure another shipment with the Western Sector." His father handed the file back to him. "Contact the Eastern and Northern Sectors as well. They won't have as much to offer, but we can't be picky right now."

"Father, I'm not sure they will send another so soon." Liam's mind whirled. "And if they did, by some miracle, send another shipment, the cost would be astronomical. We can't afford it."

"Well, it has to be done." His father stood and adjusted his suit jacket. "Sometimes, the cost of what must be done hurts worse at the moment. But I'm not willing to pay the price of my people starving."

His father spoke some truth, but what good would it do to bankrupt the kingdom now and have nothing later? Liam had never felt the weight of the crown so heavy as he did right now. And he wasn't even king yet. He always thought of his father as cold and calculating. But perhaps he was wrong. Where he saw cold and calculating, the king had merely weighed the costs and been a strategic leader. Perhaps he was simply trying to win the game as well as he could.

"I will send notice immediately."

"Good. In the meantime, you and I are the only ones who will know the date and location of the pickup. Understood?"

"Of course."

"Then perhaps Hector and the council will cease their vendetta against our current policies."

This piqued Liam's interest. "What vendetta? Everyone on the council is irritated at the situation, that's true—but aren't we all."

Liam watched as his father's eyes hardened. "I suppose you haven't heard, but Hector is calling for a total revamping of our shipping policies. He wants a committee to judge what we bring in, what we sell, and for how much."

"We already have that of sorts. That's why we have the council."

His father nodded. "We do. But the council is there for advice. They do not have decision-making capabilities. Only the crown can do that."

Liam didn't like where this was going, but he had to know. "So, what's the catch, then?"

"That's what I'm trying to discern." He sighed. "I'm having Luka pull all the old laws so I can research and get ahead of this."

"Perhaps we need to bring in an expert. Someone who knows the law forward and backward."

"That's a good idea, son. But I'm afraid that I don't know who we can trust right now."

Liam didn't know what to say because he was already facing that with the military guard and Captain Brooks.

"Then we find an expert not employed by the palace."

His father nodded. "Have Luka get on it, but do it quietly. We will go to them to meet if we must. I don't want the council getting wind of this."

"I'll set it up."

His father glanced down at his watch. "Good. You have a little bit of time before we must have another awkward family dinner."

"It's awkward for Princess Amelia, too, Father."

"I'm sure it is." His father reached out and squeezed his shoulder. "I'll see you soon."

His father wasn't the most affectionate in words or deeds, but that simple gesture went a long way to smooth out the tension between them.

Chapter Twenty-Seven

"Move out of the way!"

Luna darted to the other side of the hallway just in time to miss colliding with a young man carrying a stack of tablecloths.

"Watch where you are going." She yelled back to him, but he ignored her, nearly sprinting down the long corridor.

"Everyone's lost their minds." She muttered, but no one was even around to care or answer her.

Growing up, Luna loved when events happened at the castle. It was a chance to dress up and watch the royal family mingle with the courtiers. Whether it was a banquet or a ball, she loved to see the rooms transformed from boring everyday décor to whatever theme the party called for. It was magical to walk into the room and find it completely changed.

Now, she just saw chaos.

The Well of Wishes ceremony was just a few hours from starting, and the entire castle was in a panic. Event planners carried clipboards, marking off items on their lists and shouting orders to servants carrying boxes of supplies and decorations. A few maids lingered around the common rooms, doing last-minute spot cleaning.

Perhaps the extra chaos was because the party wasn't taking place only in the banquet hall but also in the throne room. Just like the royal couple told their wishes for their people during their reign, now it was the people's turn to give the couple their wishes for their engagement. This meant Prince Liam and Princess Amelia would sit on the thrones as the people from every class came to say hello and drop their wishes into giant glass vases.

Luna crossed the hallway and pushed open a heavy wooden door that led to the servants' living quarters. Three flights of stairs later, she glanced at her watch and fought back a yawn. She'd stayed up too late last night, finishing the necklace she was making for Mia. After their long talk the other day, she wanted to do something nice for the princess, who was quickly becoming a good friend.

Pushing open the door to her room, she nearly tripped on a broken lamp. *What in the world?*

Her entire room was turned upside down. Tears filled her eyes as she took in the damage. Clothes were dumped onto her bed, the contents of her dresser scattered all along the floor, and her picture frames shattered on her desk.

The necklace!

She ran across the room and dropped to the ground, feeling under the frame for the small leather pouch she tucked away. Her fingers slid down the metal bar until she grasped the string of the bag.

She opened it and breathed a sigh of relief as the amethyst necklace dumped out in her palm. At least it was safe, and all her hard work wasn't for nothing.

Whoever did this wasn't after the necklace, so why did they ransack her room? She leaned against her bed and carefully put the gift back in the pouch. What could she have possibly done to warrant this?

Tears filled her eyes, and she brushed them away.

A gentle knock sounded on her door. "Luna, whatever are you doing on the floor?"

She looked up to find the queen's maid, Piper, standing in the doorway, her eyes wide in shock. "And what happened in here?"

Getting to her feet, she wiped away the tears. In her haste to check on the necklace, she hadn't closed her door. "Someone destroyed it."

The woman came inside and shut the door behind her. "Are you all right?"

"Just a little shaken up."

"I bet." Piper picked up the broken lamp and set it on the table. "Why would someone do such a thing?"

"I don't know." Luna slid the bag into her apron pocket and bent to retrieve one of the dresser drawers. "What are you doing up here at this time?" She stole a glance at the maid, curious to see what she would say. Usually, no one was up in the servant's area at this time of day. Especially when there was an event, it was all hands on deck to pull everything off without a hitch.

The maid picked up another drawer and passed it over. "I was changing out of my uniform for the ceremony." She pointed to Luna's uniform. "Shouldn't you do the same?" Luna stole another glance at the young woman, trying to decide if she was telling the truth. She watched as the girl picked up the last drawer. But all she saw was genuine sympathy.

"I guess. I just got distracted."

"That's understandable." Piper looked around the room and shook her head. "Would you like me to come back after the ceremony and help you set it right?"

"Oh, you don't have to do that."

"Take the help, Luna." The girl sighed. "We lady maids have to stick together."

Chapter Twenty-Eight

"I'm not trying to question your fashion sense, Luna, but do you think black is the best choice for tonight's event?" Mia ran her palms over the silky material and almost took back her words. The off-the-shoulder, tea-length dress made her want to twirl around like she was a little girl again.

"It will be—once we add this."

A gasp left her lips as she turned around to see Luna holding up a silver necklace. Three delicate black beads graced each side of the chain, but in the middle, three beautiful amethyst stones hung down, each one getting a little larger than the one before.

"Luna, this is too much." Awe filled her voice as she ran a hand over the smooth stones.

"It's just right. Now, sit back down so I can put it on."

"Thank you. It's gorgeous."

"I'm glad you like it." Her maid clasped the necklace and gently eased Mia's curls from her shoulder to their rightful spot hanging down the back of her neck. "And now we've got to get to the throne room."

Funny how just two words had the power to crumble her self-confidence. *Throne room.* It wasn't just playing the part of a princess. That was always at the forefront of her mind, and she constantly wondered if she was doing a good enough job.

But here, in the Southern Sector, the role of princess was so very real. The position meant a great deal to the people. It had meaning and purpose. Value. It wasn't something one would take lightly. And the longer she played this part, the more twisted and tangled her feelings became.

She stroked the cold stones that hung around her neck. Luna was doing everything she could to make Mia look the part of a princess. And staring at her likeness in the vanity mirror, she almost believed the reflection. Her makeup was perfect, not a single strand of hair out of place, and she wore the most beautiful gown and jewelry she had ever seen.

For a moment, she could almost believe she was a princess.

The plan was to pretend until she could secure a way out. But so far, that hadn't happened. And she didn't know how much longer she could fake it and leave her heart out of it.

"Your Highness, good evening."

Mia jerked at the voices coming from the sitting-room door. She was so lost in her own thoughts that she didn't even notice that Luna had left. She pushed up from the vanity chair but paused at the doorway, stuffing down her feelings and taking in a calming breath.

"Good evening, Luna." But hearing Liam's confident voice from the other room made her heart skip a beat.

"I thought it would be nice for Princess Amelia and me to walk in together for the Well of Wishes ceremony."

Aw, there it was. If anything could cure her racing heart, it was the use of the real princess's name. Nothing like a dose of reality to remind her who she really was. She held her chin up, though, and plastered on a smile as she entered the sitting room. It was time to use the princess mask again.

"I would be delighted, Prince Liam."

His eyes lit up as he shifted his gaze from Luna to hers. "You look beautiful."

Her traitor heart fluttered again. "Thank you, Your Highness."

"Please, it's Liam." He reached out his hand for her to accept. "Shall we?"

She placed her hand in his and tried to ignore the current of electricity that shot through at his touch. "I'm ready if you are."

Get ahold of yourself, Mia. You cannot fall for a prince. Not now, not ever.

Mia argued with herself about all the reasons why she needed to harden her heart to Liam as they walked. But with each step closer to the throne room, she found it harder and harder to argue back. Her mind seemed to replay every smile, every kind word, every thrill of excitement at seeing Liam, and she suddenly forgot why she was trying to talk herself out of it, to begin with.

But as two servants in matching navy uniforms pulled open the double doors, it hit her.

Mia had never seen the throne room before, and really, she shouldn't have been surprised about how it would look, but for some reason, seeing the four wooden thrones with their tall backs, high armrests, and padded seats sent thoughts of romance far from her mind.

In true Southern Sector fashion, the room was elegant but not overstated. Wooden beams graced the arched ceiling, and tall floor-to-ceiling windows swept down the left side of the room, letting in natural light. Large vases of flowers graced the steps of the platform.

It nearly took her breath away.

But what was in the center of the room made everything come into sharp focus. Four separate queue lines were placed directly in the middle of the floor. At the end, four overly large glass vases stood on pedestals.

"Are you all right, Mia?"

She realized too late that Liam was trying to lead her into the room, but she stood still, rooted in place. "I'm sorry—I got caught up with the room's beauty."

He took a step toward her and nodded. "They have done a wonderful job, haven't they?"

"Yes." She hated that her voice trembled, giving away her nerves. She gestured to the platform more confidently, adding, "Shall we?"

"Normally, we would sit in the back row, but since today is all about us, we will take the first two thrones."

"Where are your parents?" She scanned the room but didn't see them around the crowd of servants getting into their respective stations by the doors and at each end of the line.

At the platform stairs, Liam offered his arm again, and she took it, climbing up beside him. He motioned for her to sit, and then he followed suit. "Knowing my parents, my father is no doubt doing something to make them late."

The sound of a door opening to their left caught Mia's attention. "Was that there before?" When she surveyed the room, she had only noticed the door they had come through.

"Harold, if we are late, it'll be your fault."

"My fault? I'm always the one who's waiting on you." King Harold didn't even spare a glance back at the queen but headed directly toward the thrones.

Liam sighed as if that was a normal occurrence. "*Ah*, that's just one of several secret passageways in the castle. Looks like we may need it later to escape my parents' mood."

Chapter Twenty-Nine

"Mother, you look stunning tonight, as always." Liam got to his feet and kissed her cheek.

"Thank you, dear." Her words were warm and kind. All that was missing was a smile. She turned to Mia, who was silently waiting beside him.

"Good evening, Princess Amelia."

Mia stood and curtsied, but neither one of them moved to embrace each other. "Good evening, Your Majesty."

He'd hoped their last meal together would have warmed his mother up to Mia, but so far, she'd kept her distance. Queen Scarlett was always polite and kind but had never tried to get to know Mia. He reached out and gave Mia's hand a gentle and encouraging squeeze as his parents moved to their thrones. After his parents took their places, he waited for Mia to sit down, but she just stood there, staring out in front of her. He quietly cleared his throat and gestured to the seat.

"*Oh!*" Her blue eyes widened before finally claiming the throne beside him.

He sat down and leaned toward her, dropping his voice to a whisper. "I'm sorry for my parents' entrance."

"You don't have to apologize."

Understanding filled her eyes, and he did not want to break their connection. He finally cleared his throat and continued. "I fear that the rebels have stirred up tension that's already been churning for quite a while."

"I'm sure that has everyone on edge, and rightly so."

"Look, Mia," he wanted to reach for her hand, but the doors opened, and excited voices filled the hall.

"Good evening, people of the Southern Sector." His father's voice boomed from behind him as the king rose and walked around the thrones to the first step in front of Liam. "On behalf of my lovely bride, Queen Scarlett, and myself, I want to welcome you to the Well of Wishes!"

The crowd burst out in applause and cheers, and Liam smiled. More cheers echoed out the door and down the hall, a delayed reaction from the first one. There were more people here than he thought.

"We are so thankful that you have come out to honor Prince Liam and Princess Amelia with your blessings on their engagement."

More applauding. Someone upfront whistled, sending a ripple of laughter through the crowd.

"Now, please come forward, one family at a time, drop your wish into the vase, say hello, and then exit into the ballroom. Help yourself to the refreshments and mingle with your neighbors before you go."

His father nodded to the servants standing in front of the pillars. In one swift motion, they cut the silk ribbon, blocking the first people in line from the vases. Liam stole a glance at Mia and watched as surprise and wonder filled her eyes when four sets of families stepped up to the vase, dropped in their parchment, and bowed in front of them.

He leaned close and whispered, "I know custom dictates one line and a discussion with each subject, but we just can't house that many people in the castle for long. We'd be here all night."

Confusion flickered in her eyes for just a moment, and then it was gone, a smile and laughter taking its place. "No, of course not. This was a great idea."

He leaned back to his normal position and watched a young couple approach on his right.

By the looks of their worn and tattered clothing, they were poor. The young woman was pregnant and laid her hand across her stomach as she walked. Her husband had one arm around his wife, supporting her while carrying a small toddler in his other arm.

The adorable little boy chuckled as his thin hand dropped the paper into the vase. The couple exchanged a loving grin before turning toward the throne. As if they practiced beforehand, all three of them bowed at the same time. Liam nodded at them and waved to the little boy. But as they turned to leave, something tugged at his conscience.

For them to be the first in line, they would have had to wait for hours in line before the ceremony even started. Which meant his pregnant wife would have been on her feet for so long, and he would have given up a day's wages. There's no way they could have afforded that, so why did they do it?

Liam had never felt so less worthy in his life. He signaled for Luka to come over.

"Your Highness?" His servant's worried voice filled his ear.

"That couple that just left—can you get their wish, please? I would like to see it now."

Luka raised his eyebrow but didn't comment further. He signaled for the next family to wait and retrieved it from the glass vase. Luka handed it over and Liam placed it in his pocket to look at later. He didn't want to appear rude to his other subjects.

Liam peeked over at Mia, but she didn't seem to have suspected anything as she was engrossed with a redheaded little girl with curls secured back in a ribbon and a braid—just like the one that Mia had worn before.

The girl wiggled her way out of her father's arms and ran past the vase toward Mia. A servant tried to intercept the child, but

Mia held up her hand for them to stop and leaned forward to scoop the girl up into a hug and pull her up on her lap.

The crowd ceased their conversations, and silence filled the large room. People twisted and turned to better see the princess playing and talking with the little girl.

"I'm sorry, Your Highness, for the inconvenience." The father said, bowing to both of them. "Our daughter, Ella, has become quite taken with Princess Amelia. She even wants her hair braided in the same way."

"Well, I cannot fault her there. I am as well."

The crowd laughed. Mia flashed him a grin, and he wondered about one day having a child of his own. Now, where did those thoughts come from? He was simply getting caught up in the emotions of the evening.

The mother called out to the little girl, breaking his train of thought. "Ellie, come back here."

"Ma, I give the princess my pwresent." The girl produced a picture from the pocket of her dress. "See, Pwrincess Amelia, I made you a picture."

A hush fell over the crowd again as Mia opened the drawing— her eyes filling with tears as she looked at it.

Liam tried to look at the gift, but Mia held it up against her chest.

The girl took her finger and wiped Mia's cheek. "*Aw,* don't you like it?"

Mia laughed and hugged the girl again. "I love it, and I'm going to hang it up in my room." She gave the girl a huge grin and lowered her voice. "As one artist to another, you have a gift, Ellie, so don't stop drawing. Okay?"

The girl nodded, soaking up every word. Liam had to admit that Mia had him mesmerized as well.

"I will." The girl jumped down from Mia's lap and ran back to her mother, who also was wiping back a tear. "Did you hear that, Mama? She liked it!"

The couple bowed, then headed off to the ballroom, and the

line moved again. Mia looked over at him, a goofy grin on her face. For the first time since she'd arrived at the castle, she looked relaxed at ease. Maybe even content?

Was there a possibility that Mia was happy with their engagement? His pulse skyrocketed at the thought.

"That was a really sweet thing you just did. Most royals would have turned away the girl."

Her eyes widened. "Seriously? Who could turn away a child?"

Liam nodded. "Who, indeed?"

The next two hours went by in a blur as one person after another filled the throne room and dropped their wish into the vase before them. He would glance over at Mia every now and then to see if she grew tired of the parade of people. But she held a smile for each one.

"We've almost made it to the end." He said as the line slowly dwindled to a few more families.

"And we didn't even have to use the secret passage."

"You're right, we didn't."

As the last person turned to leave the throne room, he reached for the wish in his pocket and pulled it open.

A neat but tiny script filled the center of the page. "We wish you nothing but the same happiness we've found in each other. May your eyes be opened to what is really going on in your sector. If you want to know more, meet me at the old chapel tomorrow at dawn."

Chapter Thirty

The early morning sky cast pinks and purples across the sky, slowly lighting the road to the chapel. Liam parked about a block away from the building and quickly shut the car and lights off.

Climbing out of the vehicle, he raised the hood of his jacket over his head and walked to the sidewalk, keeping in the building's shadows as much as possible. He dressed in simple jeans and a cotton T-shirt, leaving his business attire in his closet. Hopefully, the jacket and plain clothes would shift any focus away from him if anyone was out and about on the streets.

He didn't know why this man left such a cryptic note in the vase of wishes, but he knew he couldn't ignore the message. Not when there was a chance he could learn something about what was going on with these rebels.

It was probably stupid, but he didn't alert anyone to his departure from the castle. Not even Luka knew he was gone. The note didn't say to come alone, but for some reason, it felt important to do so. Like this was something that he needed to learn on his own. Besides, Liam didn't know who he could trust in the guard, and he couldn't jeopardize the entire plan for the next shipment of goods due to arrive in a few days.

The only thing he couldn't figure out was why the chapel? Why use a place that was completely off limits? Perhaps that was the answer right there. No one would think to look for the prince having a secret meeting within an outlawed building.

Which was another tick mark for the stupid category. No one would think to look for him there—if something were to happen. But nothing in the man's demeanor from the Well of Wishes ceremony alerted Liam of a threat.

The chapel came into view, and he would be standing in front of the door in just a few more steps.

Liam took a moment to study the building. The sagging roof and chipped paint made for a sad image. What would his ancestors think if they realized their hard work and years of caring for the once-beautiful building would result in this?

Would they still be proud of their family legacy? They had come a long way on one hand—building the chapel with their bare hands—to now, ruling an entire portion of the former USA. But, on the other hand, the Southern Sector denied the whole reason for the chapel's existence.

It was a moral conundrum that Liam had never been able to work out in his mind. In many ways, he was just like the abandoned chapel. While he embraced his family's faith on the inside, he denied it on the outside.

Footsteps creaked on the other side of the door, and Liam had just seconds to decide what he would do. Go in and hope to learn something important for the Sector, or go back to the safety of the castle? And what? Hide his head in the sand and hope the rebel situation would all work out?

He couldn't do that. He wouldn't do the very thing that the council accused his family of doing. Liam climbed the chapel steps and pushed open the door. It groaned against the years of neglect.

"I didn't know if you would show up." The man from last night's ceremony rose from one of the wooden pews and bowed his head. "Your Highness."

Liam closed the door behind him, flinching as it scratched along the floor. "For a moment, I didn't either." He quickly lowered his hood and then extended his hand. "Mr. ..."

The man's calloused hand pumped his up and down. "Burke Parry."

"Mr. Parry."

"Please, Your Highness, it's Burke." The young man dropped his hand and gestured to the pew. "Would you like to sit down?"

"I need to get back before I'm missed." Liam shifted his weight to his left leg. "Why did you ask me here, Burke?"

Surprise flickered across the man's face at Liam's bluntness. "Of course. I work at the warehouse, Your Highness, stacking boxes and taking inventory."

"How long have you worked there?" Liam's mind whirled in several different directions at the new information. Was there something wrong at the warehouse?

"My father got me on after I turned eighteen. I've been there for five years." Burke hesitated, apprehension showing in more than just his tone. "My father has worked there his whole life."

Liam needed to put the man at ease. He came into the chapel on edge, unsure of what he would find. But Burke wasn't a threat. He was loyal. That much Liam could tell from their short meeting.

"Burke, don't worry. What you tell me is in confidence. I'm only here to help, not to take away your or your father's job."

"Thank you, sir. But with all due respect, you're not the one I'm worried about. I know that you care about your people. Other workers have talked about your efforts to stop the rebels."

"Then, who are you worried about?"

"I'm afraid the rebels will not stop with just raiding the convoys." Burke sighed. "I don't say much at work. I just go and do my job, then go home to my family." His gaze turned more intense. "They are my priority, Your Highness."

"As they should be, Burke." Liam gave him a nod. "Please continue."

"Since I keep to myself, I'm easily overlooked. And people talk. At first, it was just about normal aggravation for the situation. But lately, that grumbling has turned more bent on revenge. Your Highness, workers are talking about taking matters into their own hands."

A knot of fear curled up in his stomach at Burke's words. This was worse than his people thinking he couldn't take care of them. His own guard couldn't find the rebels, so what did the workers think they could do? "What are they planning to do, Burke?"

"Something the rebels are already doing, but on a much grander scale." Burke ran a hand over his cropped hair. "Instead of taking a little bit of food and handing it out to the people, they are planning to take the whole warehouse hostage."

"When?" Could they even pull something like that off? Liam racked his brain, trying to remember how many employees worked at the warehouse. Last time he looked, it was well over fifty.

"I don't have the exact date. I thought it was just all talk, you know? But if it's not? What would happen to the workers? What if an actual fight happened with the guard?" Burke shook his head. "I couldn't have people's lives hanging over my head."

Liam placed his hand on the man's shoulder. "You did the right thing, Burke. I'm going to do everything in my power to prevent any bloodshed from happening. All I want is for this food shortage and rebel attacks to end."

Bells from the market square chimed in the distance—six long, high-pitched rings.

"I have to get to work, Your Highness. They will dock my pay if I am late."

"Of course. If you hear anything else, please come to the castle and ask to speak with me. I will add you to the list so they won't question you."

"Thank you, Your Highness."

With that, Burke hurried out of the chapel, leaving Liam to his thoughts. He crossed over to the first pew on his right and put his head in his hands. He didn't quite know what he expected when he met with the young man, but learning about this wasn't something that even crossed his radar.

His people were going to take matters into their own hands. They were going to do the job they felt like he had failed.

Guilt weighed heavily on his shoulders. He thought he would have time to figure this whole problem out. He believed if he got engaged to Princess Amelia, that would smooth over their shipping issues. And he hoped they could stop the rebels once he figured out who the mole was.

But Liam never considered his own people would go to such lengths. And Burke was right. If a fight broke out, lives could be lost. Because while the people thought they were protecting people, the guards would protect the warehouse. There would be casualties.

What was he going to do now?

What *could* he do?

A gentle breeze blew through the open windows, and Liam did something that he'd never had the opportunity to do before. He closed his eyes, bowed his head, and prayed in the one place he was denied and the one place he had to deny his people to come to.

The chapel.

Chapter Thirty-One

"I don't know what to make for Prince Liam for the Gift Ceremony." Mia looked up from her painting of the castle gardens as Luna carried in a breakfast tray.

"Hello to you, too, Your Highness." Luna set the tray down on the small table in the art studio and frowned. "You missed breakfast."

Mia set down her brush. "I know, and I'm sorry. I just wasn't hungry." Her stomach had been in knots since the Well of Wishes ceremony.

"The Gift Ceremony is a short but very special ceremony. Usually, only the immediate family and courtiers are in attendance. You'll exchange a gift, and then dinner and dancing."

"So, no pressure." Mia raised her eyebrow and picked up her brush, dipping it in a bright yellow on her color palette.

"I'm sure the prince will love anything you give him." Luna gave a genuine grin. One that Mia noticed she saved for when she wanted to tease her. "He couldn't take his eyes off you when that little girl climbed up in your lap."

Heat flamed her cheeks, but she didn't give in to Luna's teasing. "I thought for sure that I messed everything up. I didn't even think. I just scooped her up."

"Well, it may not have been how a princess would have done it, but I think it was just what was needed. Did you notice how much the people embraced you after that?"

It was true. At every ceremony so far, there was always such a tense charge to the air whenever she stood in front of the people that she assumed it was just her nerves. But after that adorable little girl ran back to her parents, it was like a wall had been broken down, and Mia could feel their approval. It was silly, but for the first time since arriving at the castle, she almost felt like she belonged there.

She shook her head, clearing away the thoughts of belonging. Because she didn't, and she had no right to wish it was so.

"It's all going to be okay, Mia." Luna laid her hand on her arm, jarring Mia from her depressing thoughts. "We are in the home stretch."

"Yes, we are." She forced a smile to convey more confidence than she felt. One more ceremony, and then she had to come up with some sort of plan to leave. Except every time she entertained the idea of leaving, her heart ached.

"Well, I need to go finish your present from Prince Liam." Luna grinned again, getting up from the table.

"Wait, you're making the present? No fair!"

"Don't even think about it." Luna wagged her finger in Mia's direction. "I do not have time to make something from you as well."

Of course, she didn't, and Mia wouldn't add another item to Luna's list of duties. She was already doing so much for her. "I know, but you gave me a good idea." She placed her brush in water and wiped her hands on a cloth beside her. "I will need some supplies."

"Make a list, and I will have one of the servants get it for you. But do it soon. You're almost out of time."

"I know. I'll have it to you in an hour." Mia was well aware of how long she had before the next ceremony. It was like a neon sign constantly flashed above her head, saying, *"You have two more days before you add another lie."*

"See you soon." Luna pulled open the door and called over her shoulder as she left. "Eat your breakfast."

Rolling her eyes, Mia got to her feet, passing the breakfast tray and stopping at a small cart on the other side of the room. She tugged open the top drawer and grabbed paper and a pencil. She might not be able to make an item of the same quality that Luna could, but Mia could come up with something nice.

An hour later, and with her breakfast halfway eaten, she had her supply list in Luna's hand so she could find someone to retrieve the items. There was excitement at the idea of bringing her creation to life. She just hoped the gift wouldn't disappoint Liam.

But really, what kind of gift do you give someone you don't plan on actually marrying?

Ugh. How had she gotten herself into such a mess? Reaching for another piece of paper, she started drawing, not paying attention to what it was until she had sketched out the small park that Liam took her to after their dinner date. The park had such potential with the big shady trees and flat land. She could easily envision a swing set, playground equipment, and maybe even an outdoor toy box to hold balls and jump ropes.

That is if such a thing even existed here.

She spent the rest of the day engrossed in her floor plans for a children's playground. There were even benches for parents under the enormous shade trees, a butterfly garden, and a miniature castle in the center for a playhouse.

When she was finished, she leaned back and surveyed her work. If she wasn't going to stay, what better way could she tell the people and Liam that she was sorry for what she'd done? But how was she going to carry out her plans before she left? Could she even find the supplies she needed? Mia understood that their Sector lived below their means. But didn't the children deserve a little bit of happiness and a safe place to use their imagination? To be kids?

How could something so colorful and full of life be wrong?

A clock chimed in the room's corner, and Mia quickly realized she'd stayed much later than she meant to. Luna would be here any minute complaining that she didn't have long to make herself presentable for dinner.

Imagining Luna's annoyed expression, she giggled as she opened the door and came face to face with Liam.

"Your Highness!"

"Mia, what are you doing up here?" Liam stood in front of a closed door, but he had a key in his hand. It must have been the room that Luna mentioned when she first showed Mia the art studio.

"*Oh*, I was painting." She held up her paint and inked stained hands. "Luna and some other servants helped me turn this room back into an art studio."

Liam's eyes widened as he glanced over her shoulder. "I forgot that was even up here."

"I hope that's all right. Perhaps I should have asked first, but I missed doing something creative."

"No, I'm glad you have a place of your own. I think my grandmother was the last person who used it." Liam smiled, gesturing for them to walk down the hallway. "I'm honestly happy to see it put to use again."

"Your grandmother was an artist?" Curiosity piqued her interest. "Do you have any of her paintings? I would love to see them."

"I will have to ask my parents. She passed away when I was young, so I don't remember her that well."

"I'm sorry."

"Thank you, Mia, but it happened a long time ago."

Mia wanted to reply that she had a similar experience but didn't even know if Princess Amelia's grandparents were still alive. She made a mental note to ask Luna.

"It's good that I ran into you." He cleared his throat as they stopped in front of her bedroom door. "Because I wanted to tell you that I'm not going to be able to join you for dinner tonight."

"*Oh*?" Her voice betrayed her and made her disappointment known. She quickly added. "Is everything all right?"

"I just have a meeting that I'm afraid can't be moved. But maybe I can steal you away for lunch before our Gift Ceremony. I would like to spend some time with you."

Her stupid, traitor heart raced at his words. As much as she knew it wouldn't be a good idea to entangle herself more in this fake relationship, she wanted to. She wanted to take every opportunity to get to know him more. And from the sound of it, he wanted to spend time with her too.

"That sounds lovely."

"Good." He reached for her hand, raised it to his lips, and planted a light kiss on top of it. "Have a good night, Mia."

She wanted to wish him the same, but for some reason, she couldn't shake the feeling that this meeting had more to do with the rebels than anything else. The idea of something happening to him sent her mind spinning. "Be safe."

Liam started to respond as if he would rebut her insinuation, but then he stopped and simply nodded. "I will. I'll see you tomorrow."

Chapter Thirty-Two

"Hey, Luna, have you figured out anything else about your room?" The Queen's lady's maid, Piper, stopped Luna in the hallway, a laundry basket on her hip.

"No, I haven't." Luna looked over her shoulder, but there wasn't anyone else nearby. "But it's been quiet ever since."

"Well, that's good then, right?" Innocent, wide brown eyes looked back at her, expecting Luna to agree. And she wanted to, but Luna knew it couldn't be that simple.

Not wanting to get into that, she replied, "Yeah, it is."

"Are you all set for the ceremony? Is there anything I can do to help?"

"You're so kind to offer, but I think I'm all set." Luna gestured to the basket. "Besides, it looks like you got a load there."

Piper rolled her eyes. "Yes. I have lots of ironing in my future. I'm afraid it never ends. You just wait until Princess Amelia becomes Queen."

"What a wonderful day that will be."

Luna jumped at the nasally voice behind her and turned to find Mr. Ortega grinning from ear to ear.

Just the sight of the man sent her into a panic. "Mr. Ortega, you startled me." Luna stepped back, placing herself beside Piper and putting distance between her and the advisor.

"My apologies, Miss." He swiped his hat from his head and placed it over his heart before turning to the other maid. "I simply wanted to stop by and see how things were going for tomorrow?"

Her palms itched, and she wished she had a laundry basket to distract herself with or to toss at the man's head. Instead, she clasped her hands behind her back. "Everything is great. Right on track."

"That's good. We do not want a repeat of the Way of Light Festival, do we?" If possible, his voice rose in pitch, but she could still detect the threat as she dissected the meaning behind his words. This was the last event in the engagement. She just had to make it through tomorrow night, and they would all be in the clear.

She only hoped Piper would be oblivious. The last thing she needed was the maid to ask questions.

She had to get the advisor moving along. "No, of course we don't."

Mr. Ortega didn't respond. Sweat beaded at the back of her neck, and she resisted the urge to wipe it away. What was he doing? Trying to intimidate her?

Well, it was working.

And now, she wished she had something in her hands to chuck at the man so she could escape from his intense glare.

She glanced at Piper from the corner of her eye, and the girl cleared her throat, breaking the tension. "Well, Mr. Ortega, if you don't mind, Luna and I have some chores to finish." She held up the laundry basket as proof.

It took him a few more seconds before he shifted his gaze to the other maid as if he was finally seeing her for the first time. "Of course." He placed his hat back on his head and tipped it to them. "Ladies."

Luna sighed as the man slithered back to whatever hole he had crawled out of.

"Well, that was certainly awkward." Piper waited until Mr. Ortega was out of sight before adding in a hushed tone. "What was his problem? Does he always act like that to you?"

Panic filled Luna as she scrambled to find an answer that would satisfy the maid and keep her from asking more questions. "I don't know, but he's a little odd, right?"

"There's more to it than that, though." She shifted the basket from her hip to hold it in front of her stomach. "I don't trust that man, Luna. Stay as far away from him as you can."

"Well, he is an advisor."

"As if that means anything." Her new friend rolled her eyes so dramatically that Luna had to bite her cheek from laughing. "Stick around for a while, and you'll hear things."

"What kind of things?"

The maid's eyes widened in delight. "Well, it's mostly all rumors. You know, how they got their positions, what they think of the royal family." She waved her hand in dismissal. "Mainly, I just ignore them because it all stems from jealousy."

"I've heard my share of that from the other maids." Two maids, in particular, sprang to her mind—the ones who talked badly about Princess Amelia and questioned how Luna became her maid.

How could she have been so blind? Could it really be that simple? But now that she heard Piper talking about rumors and jealousy, the pieces of the puzzle finally clicked together. Were the maids so jealous of Luna that they trashed her room and stole the lantern?

This whole time, she feared it had been Mr. Ortega just messing with her. But that made no sense. What would he gain from stealing the lantern? Absolutely nothing. He was the one who was forcing her to make sure Mia's true identity didn't come out.

"This has been a fun distraction, but I need to get going." Piper's smile vanished quickly, and she leaned forward. "But, Luna, be careful around Mr. Ortega. He's got a nasty temper."

Curiosity made Luna want to ask how Piper knew that, but she'd already held the girl longer than she should have. Any more lingering in the hallway would end up with both of them getting in trouble should anyone else come by. Instead, she nodded and waved as the maid left.

Taking a moment to calm her thoughts, Luna smoothed out her apron, walked to Mia's bedroom door, and pushed it open. The servants had brought her craft supplies that Mia had asked for, and Luna wanted to see how her project was coming along.

"You have the gift finished yet?" she called out, but Mia wasn't in the sitting room. Perhaps she had already gone to bed. If that was the case, she hadn't used the intercom to ask Luna for help. She tapped lightly on the bedroom door, and it swung open. "Mia?

She peeked into the room, but the girl wasn't on the bed either. For a moment, Luna wondered if Mia was back in the art studio—or worse—that she had fled the palace.

Luna didn't believe that Mia would do something like that. They promised they would help each other. She surveyed the room and sighed. There, sitting at the writing desk, was Mia, her head on her arm, clutching what must be Liam's gift in her hand. If Luna strained, she could barely make out a soft snore coming from the girl.

"Mia." She gently shook her shoulder. "Wake up."

"Luna!" She bolted, nearly dropping her present in the process. "What time is it? You scared me."

"It's almost dinnertime. I came by to help you get ready."

"I must have fallen asleep." She placed the item on her desk and rubbed the back of her neck. "If you don't mind, Luna, I'm going to just order a food tray and go to bed early."

"Are you ill?"

"No, I'm just tired and sore."

"Well, I guess falling asleep at your desk will do that." Luna went to the dresser, pulled out a nightgown, and then helped unzip Mia's dress. "If you're sure, I will get you something to eat."

"Yes, I'm sure. Thank you, Luna."

Luna nodded and headed to the door, but doubt halted her steps. She whirled around. "You're not going to leave, are you, Mia?"

The girl's eyes widened. "Why would you ask me that?"

"I just had this nagging feeling that I would come up here, and you would be gone."

"I can't say that I haven't thought about it. I'm not a princess, Luna."

"We've talked about this before and said we would help each other. I'm counting on you, Mia." Luna tried to keep her voice neutral, but she was failing miserably.

Mia got up from the desk and threw her arms around Luna, pulling her into a hug. "I know, and I wouldn't have made it this far without you."

Luna pulled back from the embrace. "That's not a promise."

"Why would I leave before I give Liam my gift?" Mia smiled. "I've been working on it all day."

Luna knew that was probably the closest of a promise that she was going to get tonight. She didn't know why she felt so uneasy about Mia leaving. Perhaps Mr. Ortega's visit put her more on edge than she realized.

The entire situation was stressful, and Luna didn't know how she was keeping it all together for so long. She was bound to have a moment of doubt. As she left to retrieve a dinner tray, she knew one thing—Luna had never really had any close friends, and she didn't have any siblings. But that girl in the room pretending to be the princess of the Western Sector was the closest thing she had to a sister.

Chapter Thirty-Three

"You're not going to tell me who gave you this information?"

If his father's stare could do actual damage, Liam would have had an interesting childhood. Any time his father didn't approve of something he did or said, he gave Liam a look that made him wish he could take it all back.

But not this time. He stood by his decision to protect the young man who'd risked his job to give him information about the warehouse workers.

"I'm sorry, but I can't do that."

The king huffed. "Can't or won't?"

"Look, it doesn't matter where I got it from. We just have to intervene and stop it."

His father looked away and stared out of the car window. "Do we even have a date when this is supposed to happen?"

The one teeny bit of information that Burke didn't have. "No, I'm sorry. We are operating blind."

"I don't like that." His father sighed. "It leaves too much room for failure."

"That's why we will 'tour' the facility today and get an updated inventory sheet in person."

"So, you've said." He turned back to look at Liam. "You think our presence will deter them?"

Liam shook his head. "No, I don't. If anything, it will push up their timeline, but by then, we will have microphones installed and can learn their plans."

"I hate to ask this, but do they even work?" His father cracked a smile, the first one Liam had seen in quite a while.

"The guard has assured me that they do." He tried to keep the humor at bay as he continued. "And I've been informed that this is our only two in existence, so we can't lose them."

Actual laughter came from his father's lips. "Captain Brooks would have made you leave your spleen in exchange."

"Which is why I was able to secure them." And with that simple response, his father's amusement was gone, so Liam quickly added, "We're going to catch the rebels and grant Captain Brooks his freedom."

"You better." He shook his head in disgust. "There's no way he's behind it."

Liam looked away and focused on the passing landscape. His father's words were another responsibility heaved on his shoulders. Responsibility that he didn't want but would have to bear anyway and without complaint.

Find the rebels.

Free the captain.

Feed his people.

Marry a princess he didn't love ...

But was that still true? When she arrived at the castle, he told himself that spending time with her would just make their engagement easier. Then, at the very least, they could have some common ground to build a comfortable friendship.

But somewhere along the way, Mia became the one person he *wanted* to spend time with. Their shared dinners were something he did to ease her anxiety. Now that they were eating with his parents each night, he longed to go back to just the two of them, where they could eat their dessert first, and he could get to know the real Mia.

And if he needed proof that his affection for her had grown past friendship, all he had to do was remember last night's ceremony. Mia took the time to love on a child who most royals would have ignored. She also made it a point to encourage the child's talent, which endeared her to him even more. But did he love her?

No. At least, not yet.

That thought brought him up short, and he shifted uncomfortably in the backseat of the car. His heart was on the fence, but he knew it was only a matter of time before he fell for Princess Amelia Lockridge.

"What in the world has you so fidgety?" Father narrowed his eyes in concern. "You need to get it together before we go in. We are about to pull into the parking lot."

Clearing his throat, he nodded. "Sorry, Father. I will."

The driver must have slammed on the brakes because it propelled Liam forward, his seatbelt restraining him and cutting into his chest.

"What's going on?" His father demanded.

"I'm sorry, Your Majesty, but we had to come to a stop."

"Can you see what is happening?" Liam asked, hoping his calm tone would help diffuse the tense situation.

"I can't, Your Highness. But the convoy has halted." The man reached for his door just as a loud boom filled the air. Seconds later, screams shattered the silence as people ran out the doors.

"We need to go," the driver said, looking over his shoulder. "But I can't get out. They've boxed us in."

Static burst through the radio before someone shouted orders to the convoy. Liam met his father's worried gaze as they listened to them, directing half of the convoy back to the castle and the other half to help at the warehouse.

"We'll need more men," Liam whispered to his father. "But

we've assigned them to scout out the rebels. We won't be able to call them back in time to help."

"I think the rebels are here." The driver announced, shock lining his words. He pointed out the front window as military trucks came to a screeching halt in front of the warehouse. Armed men climbed out of the vehicle and formed a border around the building as workers brought out boxes of goods to fill the trucks.

"Those are not our people," The king stated, his voice cold. "It's another sector."

Liam wouldn't believe his father's words if he wasn't staring directly at the proof. His father was right. It had to be another sector. Because these men were trained troops with expensive guns and equipment. They had items that his guards could only dream about.

The simple matter was that their sector was too poor. There was no way his people were the rebels. He turned to ask his father what they should do next, but the king pushed open the door and ran toward the guard in charge.

"Your Highness, stay in the car." The driver ordered, but Liam ignored him and followed his father.

"Liam, get back in the car." His father demanded when he caught up with him. The man in charge of the convoy was on his radio, already passing a message to the troops searching for the rebels to return and help them.

Liam ignored his father's order. "How long will it take for help to arrive?" He was already estimating their numbers in his head, but even with their aid, would it be enough to take on the rebels and win back their warehouse?

The guard took his finger off the radio button. "The rebels would be long gone before they could get back. You know how hard it is to travel in our sector."

So, they were on their own with limited resources and means to overtake the rebels. What choice was left other than to wait them out? The rebels wouldn't surrender without a fight, and sending the guard without the numbers and weapons necessary was nothing short of murder.

"I want Captain Brooks released and brought here now." His father lifted his hand to stop him from replying. "I know you had your reasons, Liam, but I need his expertise here."

"Perhaps we should postpone the ceremony—"

"No!"

The nearby guard flinched at his father's outburst but turned away to give them some privacy.

"It's more important now than ever before that this engagement happen." His father was in king mode. His words, actions, and tone were reserved to do what he needed to save his sector. He wasn't just speaking to his son but to the prince—a line of distinction that Liam had learned from an early age to recognize.

"We have to secure our alliance with the Western Sector and come to terms with the fact that we've already lost all our food reserves."

It was all for nothing, then. Everything Liam had worked for to help the people, to stop the rebels, was for nothing. He had to stand by and watch them steal their food.

"Have our driver take you back so you can get ready. I will wait here for Captain Brooks, and we will take care of this mess."

How could he even attend this ceremony tonight when his sector was all but ruined? "I think everyone would understand that we must wait a day or two."

"We can't wait, son." He lowered his voice and leaned close to his ear. "It's too important. Our people are depending on you to play your part to secure their futures."

How much more responsibility was he supposed to take on before he cracked under the pressure? He'd spent his entire life doing what was needed for the crown and his people. Never once had he chosen himself. And now, his father—no, the king—demanded he continue as if nothing had changed when it felt like nothing would ever be the same again.

Chapter Thirty-Four

"I know I'm not who you expected to see."

Mia jumped up from the table, nearly knocking her water glass over. She righted it and schooled her features to what she hoped was a pleased smile. "Good afternoon, Your Majesty."

The Queen looked down at the chair across from her, and before Mia could even process whether she should pull it out, a servant pulled it away from the table.

"What do I owe this pleasant surprise?" She quickly looked over the queen's shoulder toward the door, but Liam was nowhere in sight.

"I think we can cut short the pleasantries. We will be family, after all." Queen Scarlett gestured to Mia's chair. "Join me, please."

There wasn't anything else she could say, so she reclaimed her seat at the table. A refreshing breeze played with the strands of curls hanging down around her face. She resisted the urge to tuck them behind her ears.

"I can see why you and Liam enjoy eating out here." A genuine smile lifted the corner of her lips. "I've always enjoyed the garden."

"Liam told me you love roses, and I can see why. It's so peaceful out here."

Queen Scarlett's eyes lit up. "I am rather proud of the rose garden. If I had my way, I would stay out here all the time."

"Well, we have that in common. My fingers have wanted to paint the garden since I arrived."

"Liam mentioned that you're using the art studio."

"He did?"

"Yes."

Queen Scarlett didn't elaborate any further, and Mia had no idea if she liked the idea of her using the studio or not.

The conversation died off, and neither did anything to reinstate it. Every now and then, one of them would sip from their glass or look around the garden. When Mia's gaze met the queen's, she would give her a polite smile to which the queen would return.

Where are you, Liam? I don't know how much more I can take of this.

Finally, after what seemed like hours, a servant brought two plates of food and set them down in front of each of them. Queen Scarlett reached for a napkin and draped it across her lap. Mia's hope quenched in one graceful movement of the queen's hand. Liam wasn't coming to lunch after all.

But it wasn't until Mia had her napkin placed and picked up her fork and knife to cut into the chicken breast that the queen reached for her utensils. Was it Mia's imagination, or did she see a slight movement of Queen Scarlett's lips? Was she praying?

Mia didn't always close her eyes and bow her head when she prayed before eating. Not because she wasn't thankful—or against it, but that growing up, it was never a hard, fast rule to pray out loud. She usually just said her thanks in her mind before taking the first bite.

But here, in the Southern Sector, where faith was supposedly forbidden, she found it comforting to see the queen break the rules. And it definitely made her like her a little more.

They ate in silence, and Mia could hardly take it anymore. Was Queen Scarlett waiting for her to begin the conversation?

This was quickly becoming the most awkward lunch she had ever had. Even more so than the first time she met Liam. A giggle escaped. She couldn't stop it, so she tried to cover it up with a cough.

Queen Scarlett's knife scraped against the plate. "Well, do tell, child. What's so funny?"

"*Oh!*" She set down her fork and patted her chest. "Excuse me." She picked up her glass of iced tea. "I was just thinking that this had to be the most unusual lunch I've ever had." She took a sip and added, "Even more than meeting my fiancé for lunch that first time."

The words were out before Mia could even think about them. Queen Scarlett pursed her lips together. Her perfectly manicured brows drew together as she stared at Mia.

Perhaps she should have kept that information to herself, but the queen asked. Not knowing what to say, Mia set down her glass and reached for her fork when she noticed the queen's shoulders start to shake.

Queen Scarlett was trying to hold back laughter but failing.

This time, Mia didn't care what the queen thought. She couldn't hold it back even if she wanted to. She laughed again at the ridiculousness of it all. Weeks of stress and nervousness all came out in a fit of giggles. It wasn't long before Queen Scarlett joined in louder, and then Mia started all over again.

"Oh, Amelia, I didn't realize how much I needed that." She dabbed the corner of her eye with her napkin.

"I feared you were angry at first because of my bluntness."

"I think you just surprised me." She leaned back as the servant cleared her plate and placed two small cupcakes in the center of the table. "I wasn't sure what to expect when you arrived at the castle, but I'm pleased you have a sense of humor."

"Well, laughter can be good medicine."

Queen Scarlett's eyes widened, and Mia knew she slipped up,

but maybe the queen wouldn't know the reference. Her heart raced as Liam's mother seemed to take her time to answer.

"It can." Calm and serene, the queen picked up her cupcake, sliced it in half, and used her fork to take a bite. "But it's prudent to take measures not to get sick in the first place."

Ah. So, a warning it was. She did know the reference, and she was warning Mia to be careful. Mia followed suit and reached for her dessert, carefully pulling the wrapper back. "Of course."

"I'm sorry Liam couldn't join you today, but something happened at the warehouse, which detained him."

The chocolate cupcake slid from the wrapper, and out of instinct, she grabbed it, squishing it in the process. Strawberry icing oozed between her fingers. Annoyed, she let it fall to the plate and tried to remove the stickiness from her hand.

Why didn't the queen tell her this as soon as she arrived? Her mind raced with so many scenarios that ended up with Liam hurt —or worse. Mia had a bad feeling when he told her last night about his meeting, and she was right. She should have done more to warn him that she felt uneasy. But it certainly didn't seem like her place.

Mia's words came out strained. "Is he all right?"

Scarlett looked perplexed. "Well, of course, he is."

Relief flooded her, and she rubbed her face. "Oh, good."

"I didn't mean to worry you, my dear." Queen Scarlett handed over an extra napkin. "You have icing on your forehead."

"Oh, my." Mia clenched the napkin like it was a lifeline. She already knew she was in way over her head, but if this lunch was any indication, she was sinking fast. Tears pricked the corners of her eyes, and she blinked them away.

"Don't lose that."

"Lose what?"

"In our world, our titles are passed down. We didn't do anything special to achieve them. We were simply born into them. But that doesn't mean that the weight of the crown isn't heavy— or hard. Sometimes, it feels like an impossible burden to bear."

Mia couldn't breathe. The Queen spoke with such eloquence and air that she didn't know how she could ever measure up. Who was she kidding? She knew that was a lost cause.

Queen Scarlett leaned forward. "Wearing a crown means serving the people and sometimes comes with a cost." She reached over and patted Mia's hand. "Following the protocols, living up to the crown—that's when we can lose ourselves. It takes a real queen to know how to keep that balance."

Mia wanted to squirm under the queen's scrutinizing gaze. To jump up from the table and scream, "I'm not a real princess!" instead, she sat there, mute and even more discouraged than before. Mia didn't deserve Queen Scarlett's heartfelt speech.

Lord, I can't keep doing this. I can't keep lying to these people.

"Well," the queen withdrew her hand, pushed back from the patio table, and gave Mia a motherly smile, "I enjoyed getting to know you a little more, Amelia, but I have to go get ready for your Gift Ceremony. I look forward to seeing what you have for Liam."

It was all she could do to scramble to her feet and force out a shaky, "Thank you for joining me, Your Majesty."

Once she was out of sight, she collapsed in her chair and buried her face in her hands. The sweet vanilla fragrance of the icing on her fingers reminded her that no matter how much she tried, she'd never be able to clean up this mess.

Chapter Thirty-Five

Liam was going to be late to his own Gift Ceremony. He pushed the council room doors so hard that they bounced off the wall. As soon as he returned to the castle, he was immediately pulled into a council meeting. Word had already spread through the palace of the news of Captain Brooks's release, and answers were demanded.

Leading the charge was council member Hector, whose temper escalated the more Liam talked. The men debated every angle of the situation, and what Liam hoped would only be an hour or two turned into an all-day affair.

It wasn't until Luka literally pulled him away from the table that he realized what time it was. He had minutes to get to the throne room.

And he missed his lunch with Mia.

"We've got to stop doing this, Luka." Liam wasted no time throwing off his jacket and kicking off his shoes.

"Well, Your Highness, what would be the fun of that?" Luka handed him a hanger with his suit pants and shirt, and he went into his room to change.

"It won't be fun when Mia decides I'm not worth the wait."

"I don't think that will happen," Luka called back through the door. "Besides, your mother went to the lunch in your place."

His fingers missed a button on his dress shirt, and he had to start all over. "You didn't."

"I couldn't pull you away from the meeting, and the queen insisted." Luka's tone shifted with the word queen, and Liam knew nothing he could have said would have changed her mind. When his mother wanted something, she got it.

He pulled open his door, tucking in his shirt as he met Luka in the sitting room. He grabbed his shoes and dropped them on the couch. "I forgot socks."

"Catch."

Liam looked up just in time to grab them. "Thanks."

"You're welcome."

The grandfather clock in the sitting room chimed. "Six o'clock, and I'm officially late."

"I've got your suit jacket here and your present's in the pocket." Luka held it up, and Liam slid it on, patted the right-side breast pocket, and felt the small velvet box.

"Don't worry. She will love it."

"How did you know what I was thinking?" Liam walked over to the door and turned the knob.

"Years and years of practice, Your Highness." Luka laughed. "Now run."

Liam didn't need to be told twice. He bounded down the empty hallway, taking the stairs two at a time. No one was lingering in the halls, which only confirmed how late he was.

Rounding the last hallway, he stopped right in front of Mia. Relief flooded her features as her eyes met his.

"Mia—"

"Liam—"

She held up her hand and gestured in his direction. "Go ahead."

"I'm so sorry I'm late. The emergency council meeting took

up the entire day. I didn't think they were going to let me leave until Luka literally pulled me out of the chair."

"Are you all right, though?" Relief was evident in her eyes, but he could hear the worry in her tone. "Your mother said something happened at the warehouse last night."

Was she worried about him? He let that little nugget of truth sink in, and then he couldn't stop the rush of questions that came immediately after. Could she care about him? He never expected that at all. He thought maybe years down the road, they would settle into a friendship, perhaps companionship.

"Yes, I'm all right. We weren't at the warehouse yet when the rebels attacked it."

"Queen Scarlett didn't elaborate, and I didn't know if she would tell me any more details if I'd asked."

A door to their right opened, and Mr. Ortega entered the hallway. "There you two are. We've all been waiting." He raised a bushy eyebrow. "We really should begin."

"We will be right there."

"Good."

The advisor let the door slam behind him, and Mia flinched.

"He's not a pleasant man, is he?"

Her shoulders shook, and then she laughed, the melodic sound changing the entire mood in an instant. He rather liked that. "No, he is not."

"Well, Princess Mia, shall we?" He bowed at the waist and extended his arm for her.

"We shall, Prince Liam." She curtsied before looping her arm through his.

Together, they pushed open the double doors to the throne room. Conversation came to a halt as they stepped through the doorway, slowly changing over to *oohs* and *aahs*.

"I don't think I've had the chance to tell you how beautiful you look tonight."

Her grip tightened on his arm, then relaxed. He must have

thrown her off guard, so he tried to lighten the mood. "I'm finding myself starting to like your sector's color."

"Well, you don't look so bad yourself."

It was just a tease, but he would take it as a compliment. Unlike the four lines from the last ceremony, a single aisle graced the hall, with people watching from both sides. At the end, they pulled the thrones back, and a hand-carved wooden table sat in front. A royal blue table runner and a crystal vase of daises were on the table.

Images of Mia carrying a bouquet of daises flashed across his mind on the night of their engagement party. It was a kind and simple gesture that he knew was thoughtfully chosen by his mother.

They stayed silent the rest of the way down the aisle, and Liam's heart picked up speed the closer they came toward the flowers. His parents left their thrones and made their way to the table, standing on the opposite side so they could face the crowd. He didn't know what came over him, but he slowly moved his arm to take her hand. She looked up at him but didn't hesitate to entwine her fingers with his.

"Good evening." Father's voice carried over the crowd's whispers. "Queen Scarlett and I would like to thank you for attending the Gift Ceremony of our son, Prince Liam Dunne, and Princess Amelia Lockridge."

"As is custom in the Southern Sector, for our last ceremony, Prince Liam and Princess Amelia will now give a gift from the heart."

Liam gently released his hand from Mia's and reached for the box in his jacket pocket. Mia's eyes widened in surprise when he pulled the velvet box into view. Whispers came from the courtiers standing closest to them.

"Princess Amelia, I know you're an artist at heart, and you've enjoyed the process of making jewelry." He opened the velvet box to show her the ring inside. "So, I wanted to give you something I helped make."

Her gaze lifted from the box to his. "You made this?"

"Well, Luna did most of the work. She just let me set the stone." He lifted the ring from the soft pillow inside and held it up for her. "It matches the necklace she made for you. Black stones on the side and an amethyst in the middle."

Mia blinked several times, and Liam could see her eyes start to tear. His heart picked up speed again. He had to be careful, or he was going to end up losing his heart altogether.

Oh, who was he kidding? He already had.

He'd known it from the moment they danced on that first night, she spared and teased back and forth with him. Or perhaps when he took her to meet Vera, and she lit up when they walked around the market square? Or maybe it was in a hundred other ways that he tried to deny all this time.

"It's beautiful."

"May I put it on you?" He whispered, taking a step closer. She inhaled and held her hand out.

"Yes."

He slid the ring on to the cheers and clapping from the courtiers, and if he didn't know any better, he thought he heard several sniffles in the crowd.

"Well, now I don't know if I want to give my gift to you," Mia teased, her voice shaky. "I'm not sure I could top that."

Laughter filled the throne room, and Liam caught even his father laughing out of the corner of his eye.

She patted her hands on the sides of her dress and slid her hand into a slit on the side. She beamed. "My dress has pockets."

More amusement came from the crowd at her declaration, but they quieted as she withdrew two items. One was a small black leather pouch, and one was a folded piece of parchment.

"Liam, from what I've learned about you in such a short amount of time, is that you love and care about three things— your family, your people, and the legacy you will leave one day."

She lifted the pouch, handed it over, and waited while he

pulled the strings and opened it. Turning it upside down, a black corded bracelet slipped out and landed in his palm.

"You told me about your family who first settled here, and I did a little research. I didn't have time to learn how to craft a ring, but this is my version of a Claddagh ring, only in bracelet form."

She searched the crowd for someone and must have found them because she grinned. "Luna also helped me by adding stones with an engraving of a heart, crown, and hands."

"This is amazing." He ran a finger over the braided leather. Even there, the attention to detail was impressive. Intricate knots were woven all the way around. Something caught his eye, and he stopped turning it. There. He was right—a Celtic cross.

His heart nearly stopped, and his throat tightened. He covered up the tiny cross and met her eyes. She gave him a brief nod and continued. He had to work to control his emotions. Because somehow, someway, she knew about his faith and how important it was to him.

"But that's not all." She unfolded the paper and handed it to him. It was a drawing of the park. The very one he was just thinking about earlier.

"This is the children's park."

"Yes. This is where the people part comes in." She nervously talked with her hands, and her words came out faster and faster. "It's a design for the children. With a little bit of help, I can see a playground, flowers, and a spot for the children to learn how to draw or paint."

"And look at the name of the park." She leaned over and pointed to the bottom of the page.

Her excitement was contagious, and he didn't care what it took; he would make sure that she had the tools necessary to make this happen. "Park Haven."

Courtiers gasped, and silence filled the throne room. "The children of the Southern Sector deserve a space all for their own. We have a big legacy to live up to and leave behind us, you know."

Mia couldn't have given him a better present, and he didn't

care that hundreds of courtiers surrounded them. He reached for her and pulled her close.

"Thank you. It's perfect."

"You're welcome." She stared up at him. Time and place melted away, and all he wanted was to lean down and kiss her.

Her lips parted, and he pulled her closer, and without thinking another thing about it, he pressed his mouth to hers.

Loud, piercing whistles and cheers engulfed all around them, forcing him to end the kiss, but he didn't let go, and neither did she.

His father shouted over the crowd, "I guess then we'll just jump to the end of the ceremony and pronounce you husband and wife."

Mia ripped her arms away, shock and confusion filling her eyes. She looked down at her hand and then back at him. She was clearly upset, but he didn't know why. The crowd descended on them, his parents making it to him first. His father slapped him on the back and shook his hand while his mother embraced her new daughter-in-law.

Chapter Thirty-Six

She did it. Mia came through, and they'd actually pulled it off. Luna silently cheered as she watched the couple exchange gifts and the sweet and unexpected kiss. Breathing a sigh of relief, she clapped along with the other guests as the king pronounced them husband and wife.

Now, Mr. Ortega would have to back off and leave her and her father alone. There would be no more threats and no more worry.

A tremendous weight lifted from her shoulders, and she felt lighter than she had since the engagement started.

Until she saw the horrified expression on Mia's face.

No, no, no.

This couldn't be happening. They made it. They crossed the finish line, and Mia didn't have to live in fear anymore of being found out. Luna and her father were safe.

Mia, do not ruin everything now.

She forced herself to look from Mia to Liam and instantly moved toward them. Hurt and confusion were evident on Liam's face, but Mia's body language sent Luna running across the room, pushing past the courtiers who stood between her and Mia.

Mia was going to confess to Liam, and Luna couldn't get

there in time. This was a conversation that needed to be held in private. Not with hundreds of people watching.

In a stroke of good luck, the queen intercepted Mia and wrapped her in a hug before the girl could undo everything they had worked so hard for.

She reached for Mia's hands right as the queen turned to embrace her only son.

"Smile, Mia," she ordered, pulling her friend away from the royal family. "Don't ruin everything now."

"I'm *married*?" Mia hissed in Luna's ear, still clinging tightly to her. "I can't be married."

Married? Why was she using that word?

Luna racked her brain trying to connect the reference, and it finally hit her. Before the Tenebrous Era, before the entire world changed and new societies were rebuilt, there were engagements, and then there was marriage.

Now, the engagement and marriage were one and the same.

"Just follow me." She whispered back, adding, "Tell Liam you need to go powder your nose before the dance."

She pulled away, biting her lip as Mia walked over to Liam and placed her hand on his arm. He bent down to hear her and nodded.

Good. Now turn around and come back to me. It was impossible not to run and meet the girl halfway and simply drag her from the crowd. But protocols must be followed, and she could never approach the entire royal family unbidden.

Mia neared, her face noticeably pale. "Go out the side door. I will be right behind you."

Commotion drew her focus away from Mia and toward the double doors of the throne room. Guards rushed behind an elegant woman dressed in a silk gown that sparkled in the low-hanging chandelier lights. Tall, curvy, and sophisticated, the woman held up a gloved hand to the guards.

"Do not touch me. Do you know who I am?"

The crowd parted to let her by, and the royal family turned

toward the guards. King Harold stepped forward and nearly yelled, "What is the meaning of this interruption? This is a private affair."

The woman lifted her chin. "Yes, and I'm the guest of honor."

A gasp came from behind her, and Luna reached for Mia, grabbing her and pulling her close. "*Shh.*"

"We need to leave." Mia urged, tugging on Luna's sleeve. But she couldn't get her feet to cooperate.

"Excuse me?" The king bellowed. "Guards, escort this woman out."

"That's really how you're going to treat the Princess of the Western Sector?"

No one moved. Or spoke. Luna wouldn't be able to sneak Mia out now. They wouldn't make it for two seconds. To confirm her suspicions, hundreds of eyes trained on them at once.

The king snorted. "I assure you, madam, that you are *not* the Princess of The Western Sector."

"How dare you?" Her eyes narrowed, and she scanned the crowd. "Just where is Mr. Ortega? The snake. He no doubt orchestrated this."

"Luna, get me out of here." Mia pushed Luna's arm, and she nodded, forcing her feet to move. But Liam had already made it over to them and reached for Mia.

"You." The woman lifted her arm and pointed directly at her. No, not her—but Mia. "I hate to tell you this, Prince Liam, but it looks like you married an imposter." She pulled something from her bag and handed it over to the king. "I truly am Princess Amelia Elizabeth Lockridge."

Luna watched in horror as Liam swung around to them. "Mia? What is happening?"

Mia let go of Luna's arm and stepped forward, her hand visibly shaking so badly that Luna wanted to reach back out and comfort her. This was not supposed to happen.

Mr. Ortega never said anything about the real princess showing up. Luna never thought to question it, either. She just assumed that, for whatever reason, the real princess wasn't coming.

"Liam—I—" Mia's words faded, and she swayed. The crowd gasped, and Liam lurched forward, trying to catch her as she collapsed.

Chapter Thirty-Seven

Mia's eyes opened to find everyone staring at her. Well, not *everyone*—just the royal family. But the weight of their gaze might as well have been everyone. The tension was so thick she could feel it. No one said anything as she blinked and adjusted to her surroundings.

She pushed up from the couch, unsure how she'd returned to her room, and met Liam's tortured expression. Dizziness washed over her again, and the back of her head ached. She gently touched her hair and found a knot had formed. "*Ow.*"

Liam's eyes widened, and he reached to help her to a sitting position. "Careful. I didn't make it to you in time. You hit your head."

"I fainted?"

"Yes, dear." Queen Scarlett stood behind the couch and handed her a cup of hot tea. "Were you feeling unwell?"

Mia wrapped her fingers around the warm mug and blinked away tears at the queen's kindness. Since when did she serve anyone, anything? "I skipped breakfast and then got distracted at lunch," she answered quietly, not wanting to meet the queen's gaze. "I was so nervous when you came to eat with me."

"Luna, please have a plate brought up for ..." Her words trailed off, and she raised an eyebrow in her direction.

"Mia. My name is Mia." She turned to Liam, her heart breaking. "Liam, I'm so sorry."

He started to speak, but the king cut him off. "Now that you're awake, just who are you, missy?"

"Father!" Liam jumped to his feet. "Please, don't raise your voice to her."

The king's face hardened as he pointed a finger in her direction. "She's an imposter. You married an imposter." He threw his hands up in the air. "And your mother's serving her tea!"

"That's right. I did marry her, and you can't speak to her like that."

"Well, that's something we can remedy immediately." He started pacing again. "I will have the annulment papers drawn up. Thank goodness this engagement didn't go past tonight."

Queen Scarlett gasped, and Liam looked like he wanted to punch his father in the face. "You will do no such thing. We all need to take a moment and talk this through."

Mia hated that they were talking about her like she wasn't there. She set the mug on the table in front of her. "Perhaps you would be so kind as to let me speak privately with Liam."

King Herald's face turned bright red, and he unloaded his full wrath on her. "You will not refer to the Prince of the Southern Sector in such an informal way." He turned to Liam. "Now, those papers ..."

"Do not speak to Mia like that!" Liam stepped closer to his father, his hands balled into fists.

Mia looked desperately over to the queen to intervene. Pain was evident in her eyes as she watched her husband and son come nearly to an actual fistfight. Wasn't she going to do something? Perhaps she was too in shock to say anything.

Which left only Mia. She was already in trouble, so what was a little more? She got up from the couch, ignoring the pounding in her head and shaky legs, and did her best to level a serious look in the king's direction.

"With all due respect, Your Majesty, I'm a part of this family now. I'm the prince's wife." Both men turned to gape at her, and she almost lost her nerve. "Well, for now—" She waved her hand in dismissal. "And yes, Prince Liam needs and deserves an explanation, which I plan on giving him. In private." She clasped her hands in front of her. "Now, if you all would please grant us that courtesy and leave."

It took several moments for the king to finally find his words. But find them he did. "How dare you?" He took a step toward her and lunged. "Guards!"

Perhaps she shouldn't have said that after all. She jumped back, nearly tripping on the couch and ending up falling on the queen. Liam stepped between them and put his hands on his father's chest.

His tone held a level of authority that Mia had never really heard come from him before. He pushed the king backward. "Father. Leave. Now."

"Liam, I'm arresting this woman." He shoved Liam's hands away. "Now, step out of the way."

If the king thought Liam would back down, he didn't. Instead, he held his ground. "Let me talk to her, and then I will come speak to you."

"Harold, see reason." Queen Scarlett helped Mia back to her feet and walked to her husband's side. "Liam will find out what happened. But for now, like Princess Mia said, she's a part of our family."

As the king mulled over his wife's words, no one said a word. "Fine." He pointed a finger in Liam's face. "You have one hour." He stormed out of the room, slamming the sitting room door against the wall.

Queen Scarlett reached up and kissed Liam's cheek, then nodded in Mia's direction, a small smile gracing her lips. Was that admiration she saw in the queen's eyes as she walked past her?

Once everyone was gone, Liam dropped into the nearest chair, his head in his hands. Reclaiming her original spot on the couch, she waited.

And waited.

What was he doing? She thought she heard him say something, but perhaps she was mistaken. And then it hit her. He was praying.

Tears welled up in her eyes, and she closed them, trying to find her own internal prayer but coming up short. This was not the way she wanted this to happen. She never wanted to hurt him. That's why she planned on leaving before there was an actual wedding. She was just trying to find the right time to do it and protect Luna.

Tears fell down her cheeks, but she didn't wipe them away. Finally, she found her voice, which came out in a raspy whisper. "I'll sign the papers."

His head snapped up. Hurt clouded his features. "Do you think I want a divorce?

She blinked, surprised at his question. "Don't you?"

"No." He shook his head and pinched the bridge of his nose. "What I mean is—I can't do that."

"*Oh.*" Mia didn't expect that at all. And frankly, it stung just a little that he didn't specify that he didn't *want* to but *couldn't*. "Why can't you?"

"I think you know why." He held up his wrist and pulled back his sleeve to reveal his bracelet. She didn't even realize he had put it on. That hurt. And she hurt him.

She closed her eyes and let more tears fall. Liam liked his present, which meant she guessed correctly. He was a believer.

Mia knew it was a risky move on her part to make such a blatant example of faith in a world where it wasn't allowed. But she knew from their conversations and what she had learned about him that he had a secret faith. And what clinched it was his mother's slip-up at lunch. But perhaps she meant for Mia to catch her.

He leaned back in the chair. "I know that sometimes divorce is inevitable. There are times when two people shouldn't stay married, but for me—I didn't do this lightly, Mia." His voice nearly broke. "It went beyond a treaty between two sectors. It was a promise that I can't break."

"I know." She nodded, clearing her throat so she could talk past the tears. "It's the same for me."

He sat up straighter—hope lighting his face. "So, you have ... faith as well?"

"Yes."

He didn't say anything for a moment, and they just stared at each other. Finally, he sighed, got up from his chair, and sat beside her, reaching for her hand. "All right. Tell me what happened. Who are you?"

She wrapped her fingers around his and covered her eyes with her other hand. Sobs overtook her, and Liam pulled her into his arms.

"I don't know if you would believe me if I tried." She started to pull her hand away, but he held on to it. His thumb gently rubbed the back of her hand until his finger froze on the ring he had placed on her finger.

Oh, could her heart break even more?

"Please." He gently squeezed, his voice low and comforting. "You can trust me."

And at that moment, she did. She trusted Liam completely. Because it wasn't until now—when her head finally caught up to what her heart had known for a while—that she had fallen head over heels for him, and he deserved the whole truth.

Chapter Thirty-Eight

Liam woke to a finger poking him on his shoulder. Surprised, he sat up, his back and neck stiff.

"Luna, what are you doing?" He looked up to see her holding a finger to her lips, and then she pointed beside him. Mia was asleep, curled up beside him, her head on his shoulder, and everything came rushing back to his mind.

He was married, and his father wanted him to divorce Mia. And to complicate matters even more, his wife was from another time.

He gently eased Mia off his shoulder and onto the back of the couch. "I guess we fell asleep."

Luna raised an eyebrow but didn't say anything. "Nothing happened. We simply talked all night. Then I guess we finally crashed."

"Of course, it's none of my business. But I brought breakfast."

"Thank you, but I really should go see my father." He rubbed the sleep from his eyes, picked up his jacket, and hung it over his arm. "He was really upset last night, and I need to smooth things over."

"What did you talk about?" She glanced over at Mia. "If I'm allowed to ask."

"Mia told me everything."

"Everything?" Her voice cracked, and her eyes widened.

Liam held up his hand. "Don't worry." Anger simmered under the surface when he thought about the vile Mr. Ortega. "I know about the threats. I will personally deal with Mr. Ortega. He won't bother you again."

Tears filled her eyes. "Thank you, Your Highness. And I'm so sorry about the whole thing." She shook her head. "I was so scared and didn't know what to do. He threatened my father."

"I know, and I'm sorry you had to deal with this all alone."

She wiped her eyes. "What about Mia? Did she tell you ... all about her?"

"She did."

She jerked her gaze back to meet his. "And you believe her?"

"Do you?"

Luna scoffed. "Of course I do!"

Mia sighed in her sleep and turned over on the couch.

"I'm glad she has you as a friend, Luna. And for what it's worth, I believe her too."

The maid visibly relaxed. "Thank you, Your Highness. She's been a good friend to me."

"Can you stay with Mia until she wakes up, and please tell her I will be back after I talk with Father?"

"Of course."

Liam went to the bedroom and pulled a crocheted Afghan off the bed. A vague memory of Vera crocheting while he played with toys flashed across his mind. Was this one of her blankets?

He gently draped the blanket across Mia. No, scratch that. His wife.

Wife.

The word echoed in his mind as he found his way to his room, changed his clothes, and headed to his father's offices.

"He's been waiting for you." Mr. Aspen announced as Liam entered the study.

"I bet he has." He didn't even wait for a confirmation to go in. Liam just pulled open the door and walked through.

"Well, look who finally decided to grace me with his presence."

Annoyance flooded Liam, and he'd tried so hard on the way over to keep his cool. "Father, I'm not here to fight with you."

His father grunted and gestured to the seat across from his desk. "Believe it or not, I don't want to fight either."

That would be the only apology his father would give him on the matter. Liam knew he could take it or leave it, but that was as good as it would get. Sighing, he took the seat. "Look, I'm going to get to the point. I'm not divorcing Mia."

"You don't have a choice in this, son." The king leaned forward and folded his hands on his desk. "It all comes down to the alliance with the Western Sector. Mia is not the princess. So, the treaty is null and void."

He shrugged his shoulders. "Fine. Then it's nullified."

"No, it's not fine. We need this arrangement with them to ensure our people's survival. And that comes with the cost of marrying Princess Amelia. Not a commoner who pretended to be royal."

Liam's stomach roiled. The disdain his father held for Mia was still going strong this morning. But he couldn't believe there wasn't another solution to rectify their food shortages. Surely, there was another way. He simply hadn't found it yet.

"We will find another way to fix our food crises. But I'm not going back on my promise to Mia." He reached for the bracelet around his wrist and twisted it around. "She is my wife."

His father slammed his hand down on his desk. "She's not even a real princess, Liam."

"Are you that prejudiced?"

"That's not fair." His father sighed. "You're twisting my words."

"You're right, and I'm sorry." He could feel his frustration rising to a boiling point. The last thing he wanted to do was argue with his father. But if it came down to it, he would. He would fight for Mia. "But we will never see eye to eye on this."

He watched his father lean back in his chair. "Why are you so against divorcing her?"

What could he say so that his father would understand? Luka had told him often enough that his father had lost his way over the years, which meant that, at one time, he had believed in God. Right?

But no matter what Luka had told him, all Liam had to go on was facts and actions. They all screamed that his father wouldn't understand that Liam viewed marriage as a covenant and that he couldn't break his promise.

"I love her." The words were out of his mouth before he could even give them a second thought. Father's face went from shock to bewilderment.

"Well." He cleared his throat. "That may be, but—"

"But nothing." Liam stood. "I came here to inform you that Mia is my wife, and we will come up with another plan for the food crisis."

His father stood as well, and Liam knew in an instant that his demeanor had switched from parent to king. "I'm not giving you a choice."

There it was, the ultimatum. Well, Liam could use that too. "Then you will give me no choice, Father."

"What does that mean?"

"I'm your only heir. So, if I abdicate, who gets the throne?"

His father's face grew pale, and he actually looked hurt. "Are you truly threatening me?"

Liam held his ground, calling his father's bluff. "No, simply a promise." The words might have hurt him, but there wasn't any way his father would back down without something threatening his line of secession.

Liam spun on his heel and left his father's office. He would have to answer for what he said, and he knew the council would be breathing down his neck. Possibly, they would call to have him removed, and then he wouldn't have to make good on his promise.

And if it came down to it, he would leave. But for now, he was still the Crowned Prince. And he would do everything in his power to find another way to feed his people. One that didn't cost him the only woman he'd ever loved.

Chapter Thirty-Nine

Mia paced her bedroom, turning the ring Liam had given her around and around on her finger. She was married. She had married a prince!

She'd replayed the ceremony from last night over and over in her mind. Each detail etched in her memory. How the real Princess Amelia outed her to the entire sector, each hurtful word thrown at her from the king, and each rebuttal Liam said in her defense. She didn't deserve his loyalty.

But what she did deserve was every accusation and insult hurled her way. She lied to Liam, yet he defended her and listened to her as she told him her story.

Every painstaking detail.

And to his credit, he didn't get up, leave, or call her crazy. Whether that would be the case today, she didn't know. They talked into the early hours of the morning about her life, her family, and how she fell through the window.

Once she got through that part, he seemed to understand more easily how she was mistaken for the princess and how she feared coming clean. How engagement doesn't mean you're married in her world. So, she thought she would be able to go home or have time to explain before the actual marriage took place.

After that, he confessed his fears of what would happen now with the trade agreement and what his father would say the next morning. He worried about finding a plan to appease the council and feed his people.

Mia tried to tell him that she couldn't bear to be the reason his people went hungry. That perhaps it was for the best if she signed the papers, but he wouldn't hear it. They sat in silence for a while until they both fell asleep.

"June, I'm married too." She whispered the words out loud, sadness enveloping her when she thought of her sister. Oh, how she missed her. But she resigned herself a month ago that she wouldn't be able to go home again. The window was gone.

What would happen now? Would the king allow their marriage to stay intact? And could she go through with it knowing that she was causing more harm than good to the people of the Southern Sector?

The door to her bedroom opened and closed, and Luna carried in a washcloth. "For your eyes."

She accepted the cold cloth and sat on the couch. "Thank you for bringing up breakfast as well. I don't think I could have handled having breakfast this morning with Liam's parents."

Luna scrunched up her nose and took a seat beside her. "No, that would have most likely ended in disaster."

"Thanks for not sugarcoating it." She sighed, leaning back and placing the cloth on her eyes. "They probably hate me now."

"I'm sure they don't hate you."

"You saw how mad King Harold was last night."

"True." There was a pause, and Mia lifted a corner of the rag to see Luna stand up. "But I also saw how much he defended you. Come on, you may not be taking meals with the family yet, but we still need to make you presentable. Did you fix your own hair?"

Mia laughed and pulled the cloth from her eyes. "If you call throwing it up in a messy bun a hairstyle, then yes, I did."

"Do girls actually wear their hair like this?"

"Sometimes."

Luna shook her head and pulled her up from the couch to the vanity stool. She tried to pull her hair down from the bun, but Mia reached up and did it for her.

"I don't know how you managed to do that." Luna reached for a brush.

"Luna, have you talked to your father yet?"

"Yes. He was upset that I didn't trust him enough to tell him what was happening."

Luna grabbed a ribbon off the vanity top. "But that's not what happened, though. I did trust him—I was just trying to protect him."

"I'm sure he knows that. Just give him some time."

"He did say that Mr. Ortega must have slipped out of the castle shortly after Princess Amelia arrived. They are sending a letter to the Western Sector in hopes he will try to return there."

"I doubt he will, though." Mia shuddered. "He's probably hiding somewhere, waiting until he can strike again."

Nodding, Luna took a step backward. "There. So much better than the bird nest you had on top of your head."

"Hey, I liked that bird nest. All that was missing was fuzzy pajamas, a bowl of ice cream, and a movie marathon."

Luna tilted her head to the side. "Ice cream, I know. But what is a movie marathon?"

"It's where you watch several movies back-to-back. Preferably, rom-coms."

Luna laughed. "Rom coms? Are you just making up words now?"

"Romantic comedies." She racked her brain to try to come up with a better way to explain it. "You said you've seen a tablet before?"

"Yes."

"Okay, well, think of a tablet, but it's bigger." She extended her arms to show her. "And it's basically a play, but instead of the stage, it's filmed and projected on the screen."

"Wow." Luna shook her head. "That sounds complicated. And you would just sit and watch them?"

"Yes."

"Who had time for that?"

Huh? Mia had never really thought about it like that before. "Well, I guess it sounds kind of silly here, doesn't it?"

"I didn't mean to make you sad." Luna frowned. "I suppose I never thought about how homesick you are."

First, she was missing June like crazy, and now Luna was bringing up homesickness. Mia had tried to push all that out of her mind when she first arrived and couldn't find the window. Instead, she focused all her energy on pretending she was Amelia. But now, with that cover blown, everything else came rushing in at full speed.

"Well. Looks like I'm stuck here." She shrugged her shoulders, and the dam of tears she'd been holding back finally shattered into a million little pieces. "And I'm married to someone under false pretenses. No, a business deal, actually."

She collapsed on the bed, barely able to get her words out between her sobs. "But I'm fine. It'll all be fine. I mean, who cares that I wanted to marry for love, anyway."

"Oh, Mia." Luna climbed onto the bed beside her and wrapped her arms around her. Mia leaned into the comfort. She cried, letting all the worry, heartache, and grief she'd held back for so long escape. "Do you love Liam?"

"I don't know—I—" Mia pulled away from her friend and wiped her eyes. "I mean, I thought I was falling for him, but what if I was just caught up in the moment, you know?"

"You don't have to figure everything out just yet."

"I just thought that when I did get married one day, I would have already been in love. Liam's had time to wrap his head around this. But arranged marriages and trade deals are not part of my world."

"You're right. They are a part of mine."

Mia looked up to find Liam standing in her bedroom doorway, his hands in his pockets.

"Liam." His name came out in a whoosh of air. "What are you doing here?"

"I thought we could maybe take a walk."

"A walk?"

"Yeah, through the garden. I could use some fresh air."

Her heart thudded in her chest. Is this when he comes to tell her that he couldn't talk his father out of the divorce? Was he leaving her? Or would he force her to leave? "That sounds nice."

She followed him out of the room, down the halls, and into the garden. Fall was heavy in the air now, and it wouldn't be long before the temperatures turned colder. She rubbed her arms against the chill.

"Are you cold? We can go back in?"

"No, I'm fine."

He held out his hand for her, and she took it, entwining her fingers around his. It was simply a gesture, but one that soothed her aching heart.

"I'm afraid to ask—but what did your father say?"

"About what I expected." Liam sighed. "He gave me an ultimatum, and I gave him one back."

"What do you mean?"

"He demanded that we divorce, and I told him that if he were going to force that, then I would abdicate the throne."

Mia gasped and stopped, dropping his hand. "Liam, you can't be serious."

"He's not going to go through with that, Mia. He cares about his lineage too much."

"But what if he does?" Mia folded her arms across her chest. "I cannot come between you and your family. I will not make you choose me or them."

"You *are* my family now." Liam reached up and cupped her cheek. "And you're not making me choose. I'm just adding you to mine."

He leaned down and gently kissed her forehead. "I'm going to figure out how to save my people and keep my marriage promise to you. No matter how long it takes."

Chapter Forty

Two weeks.

Three weeks.

A month.

The weeks rushed by in a whirlwind as Liam's days all comprised the same routine. He awoke each morning, had an unbearably awkward breakfast with his parents and Mia, and then spent the day in meetings. One right after the other. Sometimes with the council, sometimes with the experts on the law that his father secretly brought in to prepare them for whatever Hector and the council tried to throw their way.

Princess Amelia, the real princess of the Western Sector, stayed on as a guest in the castle. Taking up residence in the same hallway as the rest of the family and joining them every evening for dinner. Why she didn't leave was beyond him, but he was sure his father had something to do with it. Most likely hoping Liam would come to his senses and divorce Mia.

Thoughts of his wife brought a wave of guilt crashing over him. Since their chat in the garden, they'd had little to no time to spend together. Liam was consumed with the rebels and trying to find out who was behind the attack on the warehouse. Their marriage was still in name only, so they didn't even share a room, and Liam only saw her for mealtimes and occasionally for a short walk through the gardens after dinner.

In the weeks following their Gift Ceremony, she had slowly become distant. Gone was the laughter, teasing, and deep conversations where they got to know each other. Mia was always kind and answered his questions, but that was it. It was like she woke up one day and decided to build a wall and block him out completely.

And who could blame her? He was doing a terrible job balancing being a husband and a ruler. That day in the garden, he promised her that he would resolve the treaty problem no matter how long it took so they could move forward with their marriage. Liam just never expected it to take this long. Or that Mia would shut him out.

Now that time and distance were between them, did Mia regret not signing the papers? The last thing he wanted was to force her to stay married. Without the trade treaty hanging over their union, perhaps she realized she'd rather be on her own than be stuck with him.

Liam gave himself a mental shake. It wouldn't do any good to harbor such negative thoughts. If he wanted things to change, he would have to do his part and have an honest conversation with her. He had to make time to see her and try to fix the damage his absence had caused. He slipped a note under her door after breakfast, asking her to join him at their usual spot for a picnic lunch.

"Prince Liam, are you with us?"

Liam turned his attention back to reality. Another reason why he had to talk to Mia. He couldn't concentrate at a simple meeting. A table full of his father's lawyers stared back at him, waiting for an answer to a question he had never heard.

"Forgive me." He cleared his throat. "What were you saying?"

"We may have found a loophole to our problem."

His pulse quickened at the news, but he kept his voice neutral. "That's great. What is it?"

A balding man in a black suit spoke up. "As you know, Hector will try to use your marriage against you now. He will argue that you willingly broke the treaty and married a commoner, thereby forfeiting your ability to govern and care for your people. He knows he can't take away your rule, but he will try to get the law changed to shift trade responsibilities to the council."

Anger warred with guilt at the man's words. He only spoke the cold, hard truth. Once Hector got into the meeting and argued his point, he had a good chance of convincing the council. And even though Liam had married a commoner, it wouldn't matter to the council that he didn't know it at the time. Their trust in him would already be marred.

"We've counseled your father to have Princess Amelia stay at the castle while we researched and planned. We'd hoped that we could still somehow salvage the alliance of our two sectors."

The pieces slowly slid into place. So that was why Amelia stayed. It wasn't because the king held onto the notion that he would forsake Mia and marry Amelia. He had actually heard Liam out and was trying to come up with a solution so he could stay married to Mia.

Did he do it because he genuinely cared for Liam's happiness or because he just wanted to secure his line? Whatever the case, Liam didn't care. He was just thankful there was a light at the end of the tunnel.

He scooted his chair closer and folded his hands on the table. "And did you come up with a reasonable option?"

As if on cue, the gentleman across from him opened a large leather book, flipping through the pages until he landed on what he must have been searching for. "We think so, Your Highness."

The man pulled a pair of glasses from his inside jacket pocket and put them on. "In subsection twenty of the Trade Law, in times of extreme famine, natural disasters, or any other circumstances that threaten the survival of the sector, a ruling monarch may make an alliance with another sector's monarch."

"We already know this. That's why the marriage alliance was set in motion."

The man looked away from the book and stared down his nose at Liam, his tone full of annoyance. "If I may, Your Highness, there's more that was missed before."

"*Oh*. My apologies."

"As I was saying, in subsection twenty, section *D*, if the alliance is deemed unsuitable and no other heirs benefit from the proposed marriage union, the ruling monarchs may temporally sign a partnership between their two sectors. Sharing the use of trade and shipping routes, as long as both parties can come to an agreement that will neither hinder nor hurt each sector's ability to provide for their people."

A surge of hope welled up inside of Liam. Did they finally find what they needed? Could he tell Mia today that this was almost over? *Please let it be almost over.*

"Are you saying that since I'm already married and have no other siblings to become heirs to benefit from the alliance, we can have a strictly business partnership?"

The man closed the leather book and removed his glasses, rubbing the lenses with a cloth. "If Princess Amelia and the Western Sector are open to this type of partnership, then yes."

He wagged his finger in the air. "But it's only temporary. There's a time limit and a long list of rules to keep each party in check. It safeguards against one sector becoming too powerful over the other."

His hope almost plummeted. Why would the Western Sector ever agree to a temporary treaty? "This sounds all well and good, but why would they agree to this?"

"Per the marriage alliance, they would benefit from the use of the Mississippi River."

Liam nodded. "True, but without the alliance of marriage, why would they do it for just a temporary use?"

The lawyer leaned back in his chair and smiled. "Because

when the law was written, the Southern Sector had governing rights over how the river was used, not the Northern Sector."

Liam nearly jumped up from his chair, but he contained his excitement. This could change everything. He wanted to tell the man to hurry up and get to the point, but instead, he waited for him to continue.

"The Northern Sector never pushed the issue on ownership because we haven't had the means to utilize the river on our side. They just did whatever they wanted, knowing we couldn't stop it."

Liam drummed his fingers on the desk, gathering his thoughts. "Let me see if I'm understanding this correctly. You're saying that the Western Sector would give us the barges and manpower to run the river, and in exchange, we would temporarily give them control of how it's run."

The lawyer patted the book in front of him. "Exactly. Which means more money and power for them, and we get the necessary food and goods to get our sector back on track."

For the first time in months, Liam's shoulders didn't feel quite so heavy.

"Let's hope it's enough." He stood and collected his papers. "Thank you, gentlemen, for your diligent work on this." He shook hands with each man and went in search of his father. Now that there was a plan, they had to convince Princess Amelia that both sectors could still benefit from this partnership.

Chapter Forty-One

How had it already been a month since the Gift Ceremony? Mia had rarely seen Liam nor spent any time together figuring out where they would go from here. It seemed as though she was stuck in limbo, unsure of which direction her life would take. The more she tried to pray and work it out, the more confused she became.

They didn't have a traditional relationship by any means. They were husband and wife, but in name only. Would that be enough for either of them?

Too many questions and uncertainties kept her up at night and plagued her thoughts during the day. So, she focused all her spare time and energy on the children's park by the market square. With the help of Luna and Vera, whom she'd grown quite fond of during the last month, she was almost finished transforming the barren park into the drawing she'd given Liam.

Vera spread the word around the town, making her restaurant the home of volunteer signups and supply drop-offs. The people of the Southern Sector might not have the best tools and fancy furnishings, but they gave what they had wholeheartedly, whether volunteering to build a playhouse or donating hand-me-down toys.

She had one more mural to finish painting, and then she would bring Liam to the park to surprise him. Mia couldn't wait to show him. Children and their parents were already showing up, eager to hear how many days were left until it opened.

That's why she was excited when she found the note under her door after breakfast. She hurried down the cobblestone path, eager to finally see Liam for longer than a few minutes so they could actually talk and try to figure everything out.

Hope welled in her spirit for the first time since arriving at the castle. Maybe today would finally be the day she could shake off the grief of not going home and start a new chapter with Liam.

A feminine voice rose in the distance. Surely, Liam didn't invite his mother to their picnic. She slowed her steps, anxious thoughts worming their way back into her mind. No, she wasn't going to give in to them now.

She took the last bend in the path and froze. The voice didn't belong to the queen. It was too high-pitched and snooty to belong to anyone but Princess Amelia.

What was she doing out here? At her picnic? She smoothed down her hair and squared her shoulders. Both of them stood up from the table, and Liam caught sight of her. He grinned and waved her over.

Princess Amelia stopped and blocked her path. "Good afternoon, Mia."

Mia curtsied, even though she didn't want to. The princess had been incredibly rude to her ever since she called her out, and she couldn't blame her for that. But she took it a step further by making sure she was at every dinner, sitting directly across from Liam and smirking whenever Mia looked her way.

"Good afternoon, Princess Amelia."

"I didn't mean to interrupt your little picnic. But Liam and I had some business to attend to."

"Is that right?"

"Yes, I think things are finally going in my favor now." She beamed. "I foresee a beautiful relationship moving forward."

With that, the princess brushed past her, leaving Mia feeling like an unwanted third wheel. What did she mean by relationship? Was Liam going back on what he promised and let his father file the papers? She shouldn't be that surprised after all she'd done, but a tiny part of her still thought he wanted to be with her.

That he wanted her.

"Mia, I thought we'd start with dessert first. It's cheesecake, your favorite."

Tears pricked the corners of her eyes, and she didn't want to cry in front of him. She couldn't do that again. She didn't want him to know that the princess got under her skin and shredded whatever bit of self-confidence she was desperately holding onto.

"Liam, I'm suddenly not feeling well. Would you mind if we took a rain check?"

"Are you all right? What's wrong?" Concern lined his words, causing the sting of her doubts to hurt worse.

"*Um* ..." She touched her forehead. "I'll be okay. I think I just need to lie down for a little while."

"If you're sure ..." He sounded anything but certain. "Let me walk you back. I wanted to talk with you about something."

"No." It came out much harsher than she meant. "It's fine. I can manage. I'll see you at dinner, okay?"

"Okay."

Before he could say anything else, she turned and hurried back down the path toward the castle. Tears blinded her vision, but she pressed on, doing her best not to stop and go back. She couldn't bear the thought of him walking her back and telling her he had changed his mind. If he was going to do that, she needed time to prepare herself, to steal away her feelings, and bury them deep down so she could walk away without emotion getting the best of her.

She needed time.

On impulse, she bypassed the door to the family suites and exited the castle through the servant's entrance. She couldn't stand the thought of hiding out in her room. She wanted blue skies and open air to wrestle with her thoughts.

She needed to pick up her brush and sort through it all with a blank canvas and paint. Well—in this case, the side of the building nestled beside the park.

Usually, a guard accompanied her into town, but she didn't mind being alone this time. It was nice for a change to not have to pretend she knew what was expected of her as a royal.

Mia passed Vera's restaurant, then turned around to climb the stairs to go in. She'd passed on lunch with Liam and had a growling stomach to show for it.

She opened the door, ready to see smiling faces around her. But it was empty. Her gaze checked the clock on the far wall, and sure enough, it was still lunchtime. The walk hadn't taken as long as she thought.

Where is everyone?

"Vera?" she called out, but no answer. "Hello?" She wove her way through the cluttered dining room tables and headed for the kitchen. Surely, Vera was back there. She stepped through the swinging door and came to a halt.

Vera was there all right, surrounded by several men in military uniforms and not those that the Southern Sector Guard wore.

"What do we have here?" A man to her right stepped away from Vera and acknowledged her. "Aren't you far away from home?"

"Princess Mia, why don't you come back in a little while when we're open?" The older woman's words seemed distant and cold, but one look in her eyes told Mia she was trying to protect her.

"Of course." She backed away, but a rough hand reached out and grabbed her arm, yanking her back.

"No, I think you'll stay." He swung her around and forced her into a chair. "This worked out better than I planned."

"I don't understand."

He dragged another chair toward her, the metal legs

scratching across the floor. He turned it around and sat down, leaning on the back of the seat.

"Well, we all know that you're not the real princess. But since you so willingly walked into our meeting, I'm going to take advantage of that situation." His cruel gaze never left hers.

"Now, I'm going to bet the prince will pay handsomely for your return." He shrugged his shoulders. "I mean, he's still married to you, or you wouldn't be living in the castle as if nothing changed."

"Who are you?" She lifted her gaze to look for some sort of answer from Vera, but all she saw was worry. The man followed her look to the older woman.

"Oh, didn't you know? Old Vera here has been working for us for a long time."

It couldn't be. Not Vera. "I don't believe you."

"Oh, you don't?" He gestured all around the kitchen. "How do you think she keeps this place running with a food shortage and all? Come on, you look like a smart girl. She has to get supplies from somewhere."

"She wouldn't do that." Mia clenched her hands into fists, her nails digging into her palms. "You're lying."

The man leaned back like she slapped him. "Oh, sweetie. You wound me. Vera tell the poor child."

"Vera?"

The woman's eyes filled. "You have to understand. I had to keep the restaurant going. There are so many people who depend on it."

"You are working with the rebels?" Liam was going to be so hurt. "How could you?"

"No, it's not like that!" Vera moved toward her, but the man held up his hand and stopped her. She complied but continued, "I'm not working with them. I'd hoped I could bring Liam information if I got close to them."

"And since you got food, then all the better." Mia couldn't believe what she was hearing. The entire past month had been a lie. Everywhere she turned, someone was lying to someone else. She'd done it. Luna did it. Vera. It was a tangled web of deceit everywhere she looked.

The man pushed back the chair and forced Mia up, wrenching her arms behind her back. "I think that's enough talk for now. I'm taking you to Mr. Ortega."

Chapter Forty-Two

Liam stared at the empty seat at the dining room table, picking at the food on his plate with his fork. Mia never showed up for dinner like she said she would. They waited for her, but fifteen minutes later, she still didn't arrive, so the servants went ahead and served the entrée.

"Well, I'm frankly now concerned." Mother set down her fork, breaking the silence. "We sent a servant to check on her ages ago."

"Perhaps she changed her mind." Princess Amelia offered. Liam ignored her and her double meaning. "I meant changed her mind about dinner, of course."

"Of course, that's what you meant." His mother sighed, pushing back her barely touched plate. "I'm not hungry anymore."

Liam couldn't stand sitting and doing nothing. He tossed his napkin on the table. "I'm going to go check on her myself."

"Good idea, dear."

Before he could even push back his chair, Luka entered the room with a yellow piece of parchment paper in his hand. Liam searched his eyes for any hidden meaning behind his concerned look, but the man gave nothing away—as usual.

Luka bowed. "Your Majesties, Your Highness, I'm afraid I have some bad news." Luka handed the note to him, and Liam's heart dropped. Did Mia decide to leave him? Is that why she acted so weird at lunch?

He took the letter and scanned it, not believing what he read. He looked up from the paper. "Mia's been taken."

His mother gasped, a hand going to her lips. "What do you mean, *taken?*"

"The rebels have her." The note shook in his hand, and he could barely pass it off to his father. "They are demanding a ransom for her return."

His father shot to his feet, taking time to read for himself while his mother came around the table to embrace him. "Well, whatever they want, we will do it." She turned to her husband. "Right, Harold?"

"Oh. Of course." He finally spoke for the first time since Luka entered the dining room. "Luka, call Captain Brooks and tell him to activate the guard. We only have two hours to secure the funds and meet them at the warehouse." His father motioned for him to follow as he was already moving toward his office.

"Two hours?" Liam finally broke through the crushing wave of shock and got his feet to move. "Wait. This doesn't make any sense. They've been robbing us for months, and now they want money? I don't get it."

"The rebels may have her, but I think someone else is pulling the strings. That's the only thing that makes sense."

The door to the office opened, and Princess Amelia entered, his mother close on her heels. "I think it's time you know what happened to me on my way here."

"You told us that there was a problem with your transportation."

"There was. We broke down several times." Amelia sighed. "And that, of course, took time to fix. Which left a lot of downtime for me, and I heard several of my attendants talking about Mr. Ortega."

"What about him?" Liam narrowed his eyes, not liking one bit where this was going.

"I told you that he was a snake." She crossed her arms. "And imagine my surprise when I learned he is from the Northern Sector."

235

Chapter Forty-Three

The guard, who had tied her hands at Vera's, pulled her from the back of a military truck and dropped her to the ground. Upon impact, the air whooshed out of her lungs, and her vision blurred. Seconds later, she gulped in the glorious air.

"Come on, princess." He sneered at the word *princess* as he wrenched her up from the ground, dragging her across the dirt parking lot to a vast building without windows. She tried to fight against his hold, but he squeezed tighter, and she yelled out in pain. "You'll just make it harder on yourself if you fight."

Darkness overwhelmed her as they entered the pitch-black building. Someone must have flipped a switch somewhere, because the familiar whir of electricity hummed to life, and light filled the space.

This must have been the warehouse Liam had told her about. It wasn't long before the door opened again. Mr. Ortega, another man in a suit Mia didn't recognize, and more soldiers entered the building, taking position all around her and the man who still held her arm.

"You better hope he shows up," Ortega grumbled, pushing

through the wall of soldiers. "I can't believe you brought me into this mess."

"Quit complaining. You were only good for the information and have now outlived your usefulness. One word from my king, and I turn you over to the Southern Sector myself."

"He married the wrong girl, didn't he?" Ortega countered, but the man in the suit finally spoke up.

"And that's the only reason you're here, Ortega."

The door opened once more, and another soldier entered. "Captain Nolan, they have arrived."

"Finally." The captain pushed her forward, and she stumbled. He caught her arm and roughly pulled her up. "Let's go, Princess."

So that's who kidnapped her. A Captain Nolan. Mia did her best to commit his name to memory in case she needed it.

Daylight was fading fast, and a slight chill hung in the air, sending a shiver down Mia's back. The entire Southern Sector's guard stood before them, armed and ready for one word from the king. He stood in the center, with Liam beside him.

"Where is he?" The king called out.

The captain gripped her arm tighter, and she yelped at the pain. No doubt she would have a horrific bruise. Liam stepped forward at her cry, but his father held up his hand to stop him.

Captain Nolan seemed to enjoy Liam's reaction because he called out, "What's wrong, Prince Liam? Don't like to see your wife in pain?"

This time, King Harold stepped in front of his son, his voice loud enough to even make Mia flinch. "You leave her alone. Now, give me Ortega."

Captain Nolan laughed. "Looks like they want you back, Ortega." Two men stepped apart and pushed Ortega through the opening. The man stumbled and nearly fell to the ground.

"How dare you?" The King took another step forward. His face turned an angry shade of red. "You betrayed your sector. Your king."

The weasel of a man bowed. "I'm sorry, Your Majesty, but I was sent here by *my* king. I was just doing what I was ordered to do."

King Harold merely grunted. "Well, we will deal with your king next."

"With all due respect, Your Majesty, what are you going to do? Your sector is weak."

The king turned to an older man standing on his left. "Captain Brooks, arrest him."

The guard stepped forward, and Ortega sneered. "Like you have the authority to arrest me."

"We can, and we will. You're on Southern Sector land."

Ortega turned to Captain Nolan. "You're not going to let them take me, are you?"

"I don't care what they do to you."

Captain Brooks lunged forward to grab him. Ortega tried to bolt and ended up skidding on the loose gravel. "Hector! Help me! Do something!"

The man in the suit stepped out from behind the troops. "Someone's got to take the fall for this, Ortega. Looks like you're just the man for the job."

Captain Brooks picked him up from the ground, cuffed him, and passed him off to a couple of men behind the king, who loaded him up in a vehicle similar to the one Mia had ridden in.

"Well, I would say I'm surprised to see you here, Hector, but it makes sense." Liam crossed his arms in front of his chest. "You couldn't best me at the council, so you went behind my back and supplied information to the rebels."

"What makes you think my plan didn't work?"

Liam's voice grew cold but sounded cautious. "What do you mean?"

Hector pointed to Mia. "You married the wrong girl. You failed. The people will perish unless something changes and the right leadership takes over."

"And you're the one to do that?"

"I've already convinced the entire council to declare you unfit to lead the trade enterprise." Hector seemed quite proud of himself. "And per the law, we can take our concerns to the people, who will elect a third-party trustee."

"That's where you're wrong, Hector." Liam stepped to the side and let a woman through the ranks. All hope disappeared as Mia watched the beautiful and elegant Princess Amelia take her place beside Liam.

So, he really had decided, then? He was going to choose Princess Amelia. Tears pricked the corners of her eyes. She should have known his father would have had his way in the end. Liam couldn't give up his throne any more than King Harold could let him stay married to her.

She couldn't believe that she let herself hope all this time.

"Hector, is it?" The princess asked, superiority dripping from her words. "Per the law, if the agreement becomes void, a new agreement can come into effect." She trained her gaze right on Mia, and she grinned. "A partnership, if you will."

Hector's face heated. "What kind of partnership? I've never heard of such a thing."

"It's kind of a funny story, really." She flicked her hair back off her shoulder. "While I was detained on my journey here, I learned that Mr. Ortega was, in fact, from the Northern Sector. The very one I turned down in marriage right before Liam's proposal. Do you know why I turned down such an offer?"

Hector floundered over his words. "Umm ... no, I do not."

"The Northern Sector has nothing we need." Amelia's words were sharp and must have stung because Hector's face lost all its color.

"They howave the river."

Amelia nodded. "Oh, yes, the river!" She folded her hands behind her back and continued. "But do you know who controls the shipping distribution on the river?"

Hector fell silent and shook his head.

The Princess grinned. "That's all right. I don't expect you to know that." She inched closer to the man. "The *Southern Sector* controls the river."

No one said anything, and Princess Amelia let that little bit of information sink in. Hector looked like he was going to be sick.

"So, I can't marry Liam, after all. But what I *can* do is enter a partnership with the Southern Sector temporarily. And guess what?" The princess narrowed her eyes to look down on the man and took another step closer.

"I can't wait to get my troops here. By the way, we have the largest military to repair the barges and get the river running again." Her words were icy and menacing. "Because when I do, you can guarantee that the Northern Sector will be at our mercy."

Hector stood a little taller, raising his chin. "You can't do that."

Princess Amelia closed the distance between them and pointed her index finger into the man's chest. "Oh, I assure you, we can. We have the manpower and the resources to bury your entire sector if we wanted to, and you know it."

Amelia pulled her finger away from the man and looked over her shoulder at King Harold and Liam before she continued. "But here's what you're going to do. Your sector is going to re-stock this entire warehouse—with interest. You will ship more than you stole. And you're going to leave and never step foot here again."

"I don't have the authority to agree to that." Hector stumbled over his declaration, but even Mia knew there wasn't anything he could do. The guards of the Northern Sector seemed to realize that, too, because they lowered their weapons and visibly put some space between them and the man.

"We've already sent word to your king, and Princess Amelia has already alerted her army to mobilize. They are preparing to leave now." King Harold marched right past Amelia and stood toe to toe with Captain Nolan. "Now, hand over Princess Mia."

Chapter Forty-Four

Liam couldn't stand it any longer. This cat-and-mouse game had been going on long enough. Seeing her across the parking lot, bound and held prisoner, filled him with a rage he didn't know could exist. He wanted nothing more than to run over and snatch her away, but Amelia had to show her power over them. It was the only play they had to get Mia back safely.

His father stared down Captain Nolan until he finally relinquished his hold on Mia and cut the ropes from her wrists. As soon as he dropped his hand, Liam covered the distance between him and his wife in a few quick strides and pulled her into his arms. She went to him willingly, her hands wrapping around his neck, and he breathed in the familiar scent of strawberries from her shampoo.

"I'm so sorry, Mia."

She hugged him tighter. "It's not your fault."

"Isn't it, though? If I could have solved all of this earlier ..." Mia shook her head, cutting him off.

"It's not your fault." She sniffed. "I'm the one who left the castle."

Liam didn't want to let go, but he needed to make sure she

was physically okay. He pulled away and looked for any obvious wounds. Her cheeks were dirty with tear streaks down them. Her dress had several rips and tears, and the bottom of her skirt was covered in dirt and grime. "Did they hurt you?"

"No, they didn't harm me." She rubbed her wrists from where the restraints were. They were bright red and bleeding in places. He gently took her wrists in his hands.

"Are you sure?"

"I'll have some bruises." Tears filled her eyes. "But I'm just glad you're here."

He reached for her again, and she clung to him. "I came as soon as I got the ransom note. I'm so sorry that you had to go through this."

"Son, let's get her home." His father patted his shoulder, and Liam nodded. Night had fallen, and they could barely see in front of them. The Northern Sector guards were already driving away.

The car ride home was quiet, and Mia dozed on Liam's arm. No doubt, the adrenaline and shock from the ordeal had finally worn her out. He couldn't even think about how close he had come to losing her. It turned his stomach and broke his heart at the same time. He kissed the top of her head and caught his father's watchful eye.

"You really love her, don't you?"

"I do."

His father nodded. "She'll be okay. She's strong, I can tell." He gave him a slight smile of approval. Having his father's blessing meant more to Liam than he realized, and he was grateful for everything he'd done to get her back.

"That she is."

His mother, Luna, and Luka were all waiting outside the palace when the car pulled up to the front door.

"Mia, we're home." He gently woke her and helped her out of the car. He didn't make it a step before she reached for his hand and held him by her side. "Don't leave."

He pulled her closer to his side and kissed the top of her head. "I'm not going anywhere."

His mother reached for Mia first and pulled her into an embrace. "Oh, Mia, I'm so relieved you are all right." She let go and then hugged him. "I was so worried."

"The main thing is that she's back and unharmed." His father said. "And we owe it all to Princess Amelia."

"Oh, thank you, dear." His mother hugged the princess, who seemed just as surprised at the sudden show of affection as he was.

"You're welcome." Her voice softened, the opposite of how she'd acted ever since she arrived. "I'm glad it all worked out."

They had a long way to go to smooth out this new partnership and find their footing, but Liam figured a few weeks around Mia and his mother, and Amelia might just shed that hard exterior.

"Let's go in and get Mia settled. She's probably cold and starving."

Luna must not have been able to hold herself back any longer because she threw her arms around Mia. "I was so worried. Don't *ever* do that to me again."

"Believe me, I don't plan to."

Once they made it to Mia's sitting room, Luna took her into the bedroom to help with a fresh change of clothes while Luka brought up a food tray.

The family, Luka and Luna included, crowded around Mia's couches, eating snacks and drinking hot chocolate. It was something Liam had never really seen his family do before, and it warmed his heart to know that Mia was the one who prompted the change.

When the wood burned low in the fireplace, Liam tucked the crocheted blanket from earlier around Mia and then reclaimed his spot next to her. After a few minutes Amelia excused herself, followed by his parents and Luna and Luka.

And they were finally alone.

He didn't want to ask, but he had to know. "Mia, why did you leave the castle?"

She took a sip of her drink and set it on the table. "It seems so silly now."

He didn't prompt any further. Instead, he waited until she was ready, watching the fire crackle and pop in front of them.

After a few more moments, Mia whispered, "I was jealous."

That was not what he thought she would say. He let that news sink in. "Jealous?"

Mia frowned. "Princess Amelia told me she saw a very happy relationship with you in her future."

"And you thought she was insinuating I would marry her?" Everything clicked into place. The look of excitement on her face at the picnic when she first arrived, then hurt and tears as she said she didn't feel well. Her leaving the castle.

Mia thought he was choosing Amelia over her. And she didn't even let him explain what happened. He wanted to be angry that she didn't even confront him, but why would she? She walked up to him with Amelia at the picnic, and he had left her alone so much before trying to solve their problems. He didn't realize he'd made new ones.

"I told you it was silly. I know you said you wanted to stay married, but she's so elegant and beautiful and a real princess—"

"And so are you."

Her eyes widened. "Liam ..."

"Mia, I know this is not the marriage you planned—or even wanted. I know we haven't known each other for that long. But I do know that somewhere along the way, I fell in love with you."

A tear slipped down her cheek, and he gently wiped it away with his thumb.

"Liam, I—"

"Please, let me get all of this out." He closed his eyes and leaned forward, resting his forehead on hers. "I also know those few brief hours when you were gone were the worst hours of my life. I thought you were gone for good, and I realized I never want to be separated from you again. Mia, I want our marriage to be real."

She didn't say anything, and he was about to open his eyes when suddenly her lips were on his. Her arms wrapped around his neck, drawing him closer. He pulled back just a tad. "I take it you do too."

"*Shh*," she said against his lips. "I'm trying to kiss my husband right now." She deepened the kiss for a moment but pulled away far too quickly for his liking. A smile spread across her face. "I love you too."

This time, he would do everything right, including proposing how men did in her time. He moved to the ground on one knee and reached for her hand. "Mia, will you marry me again? This time for real?"

She reached forward and placed her hands around his neck. "Yes, I will marry you again. And again ..."

Liam's lips found hers before she could finish the thought, he said, "*Shh*. Be quiet. I'm trying to kiss my wife."

Mia giggled and pulled him from the floor back to the couch. "You're grinning right now. You knew I was going to say yes."

"I felt pretty confident that you would."

"You better be glad you're so cute." She reached for his hand and entwined her fingers with his, suddenly turning more serious. "This time, can we do a ceremony from my world? I want Luna standing up with me, and I want to say my vows to you and before God."

"I would love that." An image sprang to his mind, and he couldn't help but grin. "And I have the perfect idea."

Chapter Forty-Five

Liam's parents took a little longer to digest the news of Mia falling through the stained-glass window. But it was important to her that if they were going through with a ceremony from her world, then his parents needed to know the whole truth.

At first, they looked at her like she had suddenly sprouted another head, and much to her shock, it was King Harold who accepted the news first.

However, it wasn't long before Queen Scarlett jumped into full wedding-planning mode. She listened as Mia explained the ins and outs of a wedding ceremony and was eager to take the sketch of Mia's wedding dress to the designer.

When the designer questioned the white tulle and beaded bodice, the queen shut her down and didn't let her ask any further questions. Simply stating that the princess wanted this, and they would do it her way.

Mia wrote out the ceremony and gave Liam an example of vows she'd heard at other weddings. But in the end, he insisted on writing his own.

Liam worked with her every step of the way, even making sure the chef got a picture of her cake design. He wanted her to have her dream wedding, and she couldn't have been more ready to walk down the aisle toward him.

The only damp spot on such a beautiful day was that June wouldn't be standing beside her. Liam was helping her comb through research to see if they could find any records, but until then, she had to trust that June would want her to be happy. That carried her when sadness tried to creep its ugly head in

"It's time." Luna squealed, coming into the room. "You are stunning." She fixed the end of her veil that was turned up. "At first, I questioned the white dress, but Mia—you look like a fairy-tale princess from books before the Tenebrous Era."

"It's true, you do."

Mia turned to find Queen Scarlett standing in her bedroom doorway, holding a square box in her hands.

"Don't make me cry." Mia waved her hand in front of her face. "My makeup will smear."

"Well, you can't get married without this." She set the velvet box on her bed and opened it. A silver crown was nestled inside with delicate flowers carved into the sides.

"Oh, my." She inhaled, feeling overwhelmed with excitement. "It's gorgeous."

"May I?"

"Of course." Mia turned around and watched in the mirror as Queen Scarlett gently placed the crown on her head and secured it with a few pins. The crown was heavy, but Mia couldn't take her eyes off it.

"You look so beautiful, Princess Mia." Queen Scarlett's voice wavered, and Mia had to fan her face again.

"Thank you."

She dabbed the corners of her eyes with a handkerchief. "Now, I think my son is waiting for you."

Mia followed the queen and Luna out of her bedroom, each dressed in a lavender gown that mimicked her bridesmaid's dress from June's wedding. It was her one way of including her sister in the ceremony.

The queen disappeared into the ballroom. Luna waited until the musicians started playing before she walked down the aisle toward her father, who had graciously agreed to perform the ceremony. The doors closed gently in front of her, and she impatiently waited her turn. She shook out each hand, transferring her bouquet of daises as she did so. But this time, it wasn't out of anxiety or fear but excitement.

The music swelled, and two servants stepped up and pulled the double doors open in front of her. Her eyes found Liam first, and tears threatened again as she watched his lips break out into a huge smile. Then she found it.

Standing beside Luka was the missing stained-glass window.

Her stained-glass window.

It had been here at the castle all along.

And there, in front of Liam's parents, her friends, and God, they pledged their love to each other. Then they went to the other side of the ballroom for the reception, and she got to dance the first dance with Liam.

When the song ended, Liam pulled her away from the crowd. "I have something else for you."

"What? You've done so much already. This wedding was everything I dreamed of."

He pulled her close and kissed her. "I'm glad, but it's not over yet."

She nearly squealed in delight. "What else is there?"

He brought her in front of the window. "You've taught me so much, but one of the things I'm most grateful for is that you've connected me back to my roots. This window has always been in my family, and I didn't think much about it—I just made sure it was safely hidden away. But then you talked so much about leaving a legacy that I had to go back and do some research on my own family history."

He picked up a box beside the window and opened it. "When they pulled the window out of the chapel, my ancestors found this. It's all the items from couples who came before us and said their vows in front of this window."

"Are you serious?" She reached out and picked up each item —a pocket watch, a locket, a charm bracelet, and a letter. Mia carefully looked at all the trinkets and tried to imagine what each ceremony would have looked like. "This is amazing, Liam."

"I thought so, too, and I wanted to suggest we do the same. It will take some time, but I want to restore and reopen the chapel."

"I love that idea."

"Good, because I have a gift for you."

She shook her head. "Another gift? You're spoiling me."

"And that's not going to change." He laughed and produced a small pouch and handed it over. Inside was a necklace. Sparkles of colored light shimmered in the sun, streaming in through the ballroom windows.

It was a miniature version of the stained-glass window. Her breath caught in her throat. "Oh, Liam."

"What better way to honor my family's legacy and forge it with the one we will leave together."

"I love it." She wrapped her arms around his neck. "And I love you."

"I love you too, Mrs. Dunne."

"I like the sound of that." She grinned, reaching up and kissing him again. She didn't think she would ever tire of the feel of his lips on hers. "But you're going to have to have a second one made. Because I want to wear this one."

He reached into his pocket and dangled another one in front of her. "I already did."

The End

Acknowledgments

Teenage me dreamed—prayed—and hoped for one book, and here we are now. Window of Time is my tenth publication! I'm so humbled and thankful to God for entrusting me with the gift of storytelling.

Thank you to the Expanse Books and Scrivenings Press family for believing in this project of four different stories, four genres, and four authors!

A huge thank you to my husband, Jacob, who picks up the slack so I can write. I love you. To my writing group, you guys are the best. I couldn't get through this writing thing without you.

And a huge thank you to my readers for all of your kind words, notes, and encouragement through the years. You all mean so much to me.

About the Author

Erin R. Howard is the YA urban fantasy author of The Kalila Chronicles. She is also a developmental and acquisitions editor for Scrivenings Press and is the managing editor of Expanse Books, an imprint of Scrivenings Press.

She loves playing video games with her husband, watching movies with her children, and fueling her many craft addictions. Erin has a Creative Writing degree and is a member of Realm Makers, RagTag Writers, and Once Upon a Page. She resides in Western Kentucky with her husband and three children.

Window of Opportunity by Heather Greer

The Stained-glass Legacy Series—Book One

Faith and duty drive Evangeline Moore to protect her father's pristine image as a judge in Harrisburg, Illinois. Her resolve's biggest test? Dot, her childhood friend. With Evangeline beside her, Dot's desire for the Roaring Twenties' glitz and glamor leads the pair into questionable situations.

Born into a Chicago mob family, Brendan Dunne understands duty, but faith puts him at odds with his father's demands. Even when his brother James's propensity for trouble lands them in Harrisburg, the truth is undeniable. To their father, the lines he won't cross mean Brendan will never measure up.

When circumstances push Brendan and Evangeline together, unexpected events create opportunity to break free of family expectations. Will they be brave enough to forge their own path before the window closes on their chance to change?

Get your copy here:

https://scrivenings.link/windowofopportunity

Window of Peace - By Regina Rudd Merrick

Stained-glass Legacy—Book Two

Michael Connor "MC" Dunne led charmed life. He had a plan—finish veterinary school, get married, and take over the local animal clinic. Enter the Vietnam War.

MC returns home, injured, to Park Haven, Tennessee, and soon learns there's a new vet in town, hired when the local veterinarian suffered a heart attack. So much for his plan.

Violent flashbacks and nightmares pull MC away from his faith and turn him into a hermit. His safe place is the family farm, working on the old cabin and restoring the chapel his great-uncle built in the early 1900s, with the family's heirloom stained-glass window.

Nancy Jean Baker struggles to prove herself as a competent veterinarian to the small-town skeptics of Park Haven. Fighting her own demons from a traumatic past, she's driven to succeed.

But when war veteran MC Dunne returns home, wounded and wary, Nancy discovers she's standing between him and his dream.

Can they help each other overcome their hurts and horrors? Or is their hope of happiness doomed when the past threatens to ruin their future?

Get your copy here:

https://scrivenings.link/windowofpeace

Window of the Heart by Amy Anguish

The Stained-glass Legacy Series—Book Three

Lennox Malone may not believe in love, but she's determined to do the best job she can as her friend Sara Beth's maid of honor. Problem is, the man in charge of fixing up the chapel doesn't match her determination. Fighting against preconceived notions, a past that catches up to her, and an attraction she wants nothing to do with, this wedding is turning into more than she can handle.

Ty Dunne might be laid back and easy-going, but he's determined to make sure the chapel is ready for his cousin's wedding. Not only is it his duty as best man, but he wants to preserve the family's history in the building. If only he could live up to his family's other expectations—or those of Lennox Malone, the fiery redhead he can't stop thinking about. Before he can go any further with her, though, he has to convince her that love is real and worth the risk.

Lennox has built her walls high and sturdy, but Ty is determined to find a way in—even if it's a window. Maybe the history of the chapel itself along with the romance of a wedding will help.

Get your copy here:

https://scrivenings.link/windowoftheheart

Gates of Deceit

Beyond the Gates by Erin R. Howard

Gates of Deceit - Book One

If playing by the rules means it keeps you alive, then seventeen-year-old Renna James should know better. She is, after all, the one who broadcasts these rules to the Outpost. What lies beyond the gates had always lured her, but her venture outside wasn't supposed to leave her locked out. Now, Renna's one chance to survive the next seventy-two hours just ran into the forest she's forbidden to enter.

The Kalila Chronicles

The Seer

Book One of the Kalila Chronicles

Viktor has one order to follow:
Kill the girl before her eyes are opened.

For thousands of years, his job has been to torment and kill seers: humans that have the gift of seeing the spiritual realm. So it was no surprise when his brother Matthias was once again sent to stop him and protect the girl.

Now the last of the seers' bloodline hangs in the balance, as the estranged demon and angel brothers are forced to work together to save a girl's life and escape to the sanctuary city of Bethesda.

Get your copy here: scrivenings.link/theseer

The Soul Searcher

Book Two of the Kalila Chronicles

Elnora's parents gave her one rule:
Stay hidden away at all costs.

Elnora Scott is used to her survival depending on the decisions of others. Locked away in her safe house, it is easy to follow her parents' dying wishes until an angel, demon, and seer show up on her doorstep. Now, waking up in a dirty cell, she wishes she would have gone with them when she had the chance, because the ones who unknowingly ushered the kidnapper to her location may be the only ones who can save her now.

When Thea learns that Elnora may be in danger, she doesn't hesitate to find her. Thea thought stepping through the portal would be her greatest obstacle, but it only reveals a more sinister threat.

Get your copy here: scrivenings.link/thesoulsearcher

The Silencer

Book Three of The Kalila Chronicles

Sam's parents asked him to do the unthinkable:
And it cost him everything.

When Sam Hart was forced to walk away from everything and everyone he knew, The Kalila became his new home. He thought he could keep the past buried but after an unexpected visit from his brother, a family secret is revealed.

Already reeling from a murder of one of their own, an unimaginable chain of events leaves everyone questioning each other's loyalty. Will Sam, Viktor, and Matthias be able to stop this newest threat before they lose another?

Get your copy here: scrivenings.link/thesilencer

You May Also Like …

The Whisperer's Wish by Janilise Lloyd

2023 Christy Award Finalist

For sixteen years, Laurelin Moore has been keeping a secret. She is a whisperer, and she knows that to reveal her gift now is a dangerous risk. Past whisperers have been exploited for their power. But Ausland's queen is dead, and acknowledging her magic is her only chance at becoming a Rook in the Pentax—a competition that will decide the kingdom's next ruler.

Laurelin isn't in it for the crown, though. She's after the wish that will be granted to the victor. A wish that would save her dying brother, Pippin. But there are dangerous undercurrents to the competition, and Laurelin finds herself at the center of it. She begins to search for answers and discovers a secret with the potential to shatter the entire kingdom.

Get your copy here:

https://scrivenings.link/thewhispererswish

The Girl with Stars in Her Eyes by Dawn Ford

Firebird Series - Book One

Eighteen-year-old servant girl Tambrynn is haunted by more than her unusual silver hair and the star-shaped pupils in her eyes. Her uncontrollable ability to call objects leads the wolves who savagely murdered her mother right to her door.

When she's fired and outcast during a snowstorm, her carriage wrecks and she's forced to find refuge in an abandoned cottage. There, her life is upended when the magpie who's stalked her for ten years transforms into a man, Lucas. He's her Watcher and they're from a different kingdom. His job is to keep her safe from her father, an evil mage, who wants to steal her abilities, turn her into one of his undead beasts, and become immortal himself.

Can they make it to the magical passageway and get to their home kingdom in time for Tambrynn to thwart her father's malicious plans? Or will Tambrynn's unique magic doom them all?

Get your copy here:

https://scrivenings.link/thegirlwithstarsinhereyes

ExpanseBooks.pub (an imprint of Scrivenings Press LLC)

Stay up-to-date on your favorite books and authors with our free e-newsletter. Sign up here:

https://scriveningspress.com/newsletter-signup

www.ingramcontent.com/pod-product-compliance
Lightning Source LLC
Chambersburg PA
CBHW070631100726
47907CB00007B/1939